LOIS JOYNER BROWN

SECRETS IN THE STORM

Names, characters, businesses, places, events, locales, and incidents are either the product of the author's imagination or used in a fictitious manner. Any resemblance to any persons, living or dead, or actual events is purely coincidental.

ISBN-13:

ONE

How can I die when I keep on being born? I've already been born, twice. I often think about how it is that I know everything, too. Well, almost everything. I think I'll even know when God is going to call me home but, I declare, when the time is near, I'll know it in plenty of time. I really want to know so I can be sure that everything about me is in good order. I wouldn't want to leave this earth with a soiled soul.

I even know how it's going to happen. The rain will start to fall, and a sudden, whirling blast of wind will come. A tall man is going to walk right through that wind and downpour as easily as Peter walked on that Sea of Galilee, but that man won't be afraid like Peter and neither will I.

I wasn't always smart about knowing about things that were going to happen. I had to grow into knowing and had to let knowing grow in me. My daddy told me that it would happen, and it did. Daddy knew everything too. My sister Clyde, the only one I used to talk to about it didn't understand, at first, but paid attention to what I'd tell her anyway. After a while, some of what was in me and Daddy, gradually grew in her.

My brothers Willie, Carl and Aaron didn't slow down long enough to pay attention to me or Daddy so they could know and grow. My little sister Thelma and that boy, Maurice were too little to remember. They didn't remember much more than the day we left Louisiana and when the train pulled into the station in Memphis. None of us can forget that day.

I didn't relax the whole time we were riding on the train and didn't calm down until I saw Roxie Robinson standing on the platform waiting for us. Safe at last, I thought. She told us she was going to be waiting there. I knew right away when she spotted me. It was the sincerity in her smile that warmed my coldness and calmed the fear that had lingered on the inside of me since before we left. Roxie's gentle touch was as soothing as the unexpected, cool, gentle breeze I suddenly felt on my face as it blew the humidity from the suffocating, Memphis, Tennessee, summer air. My mind and body prayed for peace. It had been a long time since I had felt satisfied.

Roxie tried to hug all of us at the same time. She hugged Maurice too. There was no way I was going to leave him. I had to make sure we were all safe from Mama and Will Johnson. We felt safe in Roxie's house.

When Roxie finished calming the shaking on my insides, she helped us wash the dirt and dust from our exhausted bodies. The added burden of the weight of sticky mud between my toes was lifted and made my mind and body much lighter and ready for rest.

There is something sweet about the familiarity of clean, crisp, bed sheets fragrantly scented by pure, uncontaminated air. It can thrust this mean, old world into oblivion for however long it takes for the mind and body to be peacefully satisfied. I was satisfied that we were safe, and I was always going to have my daddy's lessons in me

to guide me safely on. One of his lessons led me to know that this time I had come to Memphis to stay.

On our way, as the trained bounced and chugged along, it made me think of how I used to put my head on Daddy's chest just to feel vibrations from his body when he talked. His voice sounded like the rumblings of thunder echoing in the distance. When he was teaching us lessons, I liked to watch his light, brown eyes light up. One day when I began to know what I was seeing in his eyes I could even see me.

Learning the lessons Daddy taught me and being obedient to them gave me a start way ahead of where he and the rest of his family, the Rickses, started. We Rickses were always fleeing from sadness and trouble but forever running toward freedom.

Daddy's father, David Sr. and his mother, Clyde Ricks were determined to keep their minds unchained from the grasps of slavery even as they had once lived in slavery's midst. Determined to keep their minds free, though their bodies weren't, was the reason certain people did what they did to them. Daddy's brother, Uncle David Ricks Jr. was like an acorn that doesn't fall far from the tree. People said he acted too proud to be a colored man. My daddy, John Ricks, had to flee South Carolina or he would never have been able to live another danger free day. One day, while running against the wind, he ran head-on into himself. That is how he came to be in Louisiana.

Daddy hadn't been disobedient to the lessons left to him by Uncle David Jr. That's the reason he insisted that I had to hear what he said and be obedient. I knew he was right, and I wanted, like him, to be free. That's the reason I listened, practiced obedience, and remain that way to this day. Understanding the lessons grew in me. Knowing them made me not have to make mistakes like the rest of them and unlike my daddy, I didn't run against the wind but ran right through it and unlike him, I didn't run head-on into myself.

Boarding that train to Memphis, leading the rest of them didn't happen all by itself, either. Whatever was guiding and pushing me forward then is with me to this very day, keeping me free. When I talk to my own children about the day we got here, I let them know about the time when we were leaving Louisiana and how it wasn't the end of all our sadness and trouble. Bad times were just beginning. It must have been like how my daddy felt when he came to Louisiana from South Carolina.

I tell the children how I knew when freedom's grasp began to embrace me as I looked from the train window and couldn't see familiar things I was leaving behind. Groves of trees appeared thicker. My eyes couldn't locate trees I'd known well enough to call by names that I'd given them. Standing in their places were full grown ones I'd never seen before. I admired the tiny blades of grass growing in the foliage. Whispers from swaying, colorful wildflowers muffled the sound of the train wheels. Petals from tulips and rose bushes along with fuzzy pappus from swaying dandelions flew to and fixed on the train windows rode along with me. Listening to all the sounds helped me compose a rainy-day song. That's when I knew, old things were passing away.

I thought about my brothers Willie, Carl, and Aaron a lot but didn't expect them to catch up with us in Memphis so soon. My mother Marjanna eventually came too. I had to remind my brothers all the time to be obedient to Daddy's lessons. But I noticed that I was the only one that tried to remember and to do what Daddy taught us. I guess that's why he chose me to be the keeper of the secrets and guardian of our family's treasure.

I began to wonder which one of my own children would know enough and would be obedient enough to possess the family secret. But as I watched and listened, I knew the one that it was going to be. I could feel that one feeling me. Like my brothers, my other children were listening but not really hearing. I saw them with a desire to ask but didn't. My chosen child was always thinking and feeling; always asking and wanting immediate answers. Was always staring in my eyes the same way I stared in Daddy's eyes, searching, and seeing and knowing. That child knew a whole lot more than I knew at that age. Rubs on that braid so much, I'm afraid its coal-black color will fade. Caresses that locket so tight 'til I'm scared the gold is going to rub off inside a clinched fist. Was just a little more than a tyke when the questions started coming. The questions were smarter than the ones I asked at that age. Some of them raised the hair right up on my head. That child stepped ahead of the others and took charge of our treasures and began to know everything for me and everybody else. Daddy said when the time was right, I was going to recognize the child to be chosen. Just as sure as he said it, the one I chose took our lessons and secrets from me like I took them from my daddy and is bound to cherish them until its time to pass them along.

Daddy kept some things to himself. I keep nothing. I tell my child the reason they call Roxie Robinson, Auntie, although Roxie's blood doesn't match ours. I want my child to understand why our hearts go blind when we hear the stuttering, wailing cry of crickets and how it is that we hear voices in the wind and why it's easy for us to compose songs to the rhythm of the rain. I talk about how the smell of sawdust brings anguish to our very souls and how the sweetness in the smell of pipe tobacco, the pungent odor of turpentine and the feel of four leaves on a clover brings calm to our souls again.

I watch my chosen child turn to look south on muggy, Memphis afternoons. The child knows how that kind of day reminds me of Louisiana and the day we came here to stay.

TWO

I wanted a house on a hill that stood on seven feet stilts like the one my daddy built to keep Louisiana flood waters out. Memphis doesn't have those kinds of houses but I wanted to sit high so I could see things clearly from my windows and a house that reminded me of my daddy. I wanted my house to be filled with children, running, and laughing and singing like our house was in Louisiana. I wanted a husband that cared about us as much as Daddy cared. Most of the time in Louisiana, there was joy but even when sorrow came to our house Daddy could fix it and make all things better.

Daddy said children came from God. Well, my husband and God must have been the best of friends 'cause seems like they put babies in me every chance they got and I spat them out. There always seemed to be a toddler standing at my knees and a baby propped on the budge poking from my stomach. Kept me and everybody else busy. I could have done everything by myself, but my busy house was the gathering place for my brothers, my sisters and Mama. Them keeping busy, helping with the children, tempered their restlessness. But not for long.

Memphis was like a village but bigger than where we came from and intriguing enough to allow city life to show my sisters and brothers that there had to be an even bigger world to explore. My sister, Clyde was the first to venture, following her newly found friends all the way to California. It didn't take much to persuade the others to follow. Everybody left but me and Mama. I would never have left Mama by herself. Daddy wouldn't have wanted us to do that and Mama didn't have anyone else. But the true reason they all left was because they wanted to put a long distance between themselves, Mama, and memories. They begged me to go with them but never asked Mama. I was sad about them leaving, not just because I was going to miss them, but because Daddy told us to look out for each other. He paired us, giving each of us a partner to watch over. That wasn't going to be easy trying to watch over someone 2000 miles away.

There was always a hearty welcome for all of them in our house as well as all of the other company coming by. Seems like somebody was often there combing my girls' hair, changing their clothes, tucking the boys' shirts, sweeping the porch, or hosing down the steps to keep dirt from being tracked inside. Mama came everyday at the sheer delight of my children.

After Mama came to Memphis, I was concerned about her adjusting to all the hustle and bustle and the city life. She came almost every day and washed, cooked and anything else she could do. She worked so hard, it's a wonder she didn't break those long, hard nails. Sometimes I thought she was going to rub the color right off our clothes when she pressed up and down on that rigid, ribbed rub board. When she ironed, it was all day long, her stopping and starting and waiting for the temperature on the smoothing iron to be just right. If her finger ever burned from her spitting on one and touching the bottom of that iron, she never even flinched. She pressed and pressed wanting my children's clothes, especially the Sunday ones, to stand out over all the others at church.

Mama worked quietly, speaking only when answering someone speaking to her. Her ears focused on the cheerful sounds of my energetic children. The only time she wanted them to be quiet was when the darkened sky prepared to relieve bulging clouds. If we heard thunder, she wanted us to be still. If anyone spoke or moved, she wrapped her arms around herself, tightened her fist and quietly rocked. Once the rain started, I knew she was trying to count raindrops and listen for voices in the rain and wind. I'd sit close to my children as they watched her as a storm was being born. One of them said, Grandma acts like she's listening for something.

The children understood, this was the time for stillness and quiet. But not my chosen one. It's hard to stop that one from smiling when it thundered and wasn't even scared of lightning. I put a finger to my lips warning that singing a song to the rhythm of the rain is forbidden. There were times I could hear a hum coming through anyway. That child wanted to find out whether the storm was predicting good or was it evil. That chosen one, knew when the last raindrop was going to fall and bounced off the floor and had me bounce right behind. We shed our pensiveness, all of us coming alive in perfect synchrony with the emerging sunshine.

Sunshine seemed brighter following the dark clouds and rain. For us, noisy chatter after a storm brought relief. It sometimes put the children in the mood to listen to a Louisiana tale told by Mama. My children loved my mama's storytelling. They knew by now, all the stories she told had to do with storms. My chosen child had begun to listen with a suspicious ear. The child asked Mama the right questions. Mama gave the wrong answers while my heart ached for her to tell the children the truth. Daddy said you can't move forward until you shine a light on the truth of the past. I didn't want their innocent minds having to wonder about the parts Mama would leave out. I saw a longing in their eyes and heard begging for more as they asked questions about Mardi Gras in New Orleans and about Homecoming Day at Crystal Springs African Methodist Episcopal Church, our church in Franklinton, Louisiana. They had a longing to go places they'd never been and meet people they'd never seen but seemed to know just because they heard us talking about them. They wanted to see the cemetery and visit the graves where Daddy and my little brothers were buried. I promised to take them there one day. About taking them, I, like Mama, was guilty of not telling them the whole truth. I didn't ever want to go back there and taking them to Louisiana was one promise I was never going to keep.

THREE

Verses and stories from the Bible were the only ones Mama didn't embellish because she knew everyone already knew them by heart, especially, The Ten Commandments. Daddy said we must obey all ten. The one about, "Honor Thy Father and Thy Mother" seemed like the hardest, not because of my father but because of Mama. In order to honor her I needed to trust her and trusting her wasn't easy. Knowing the truth about a storm was enough for me to watch her with wary eyes. Its like some things are born in us and others are made. Distrusting Mama with my children was made. It was wrong for me to dishonor her that way and I felt bad about it.

When Mama told the children storm stories, she was unwilling to divulge her own secrets. She was good at adding things or taking them away. She didn't tell the parts that were shameful. I listened too, not because I needed to hear the story but because I needed to watch her with my children and listen to what she was telling them. I mean **really** watch her.

My chosen child's gaze into Mama's eyes was intense. The child was sensing something beyond the story that was being told and wishing to know the secrets. When the child asked questions Mama hurriedly changed the subject like, "Sit up straight" or "Is that proper English?" All my children spoke properly, and she knew it. She helped to teach them.

And mark my word, I thought, given enough time and space, everything will be revealed. This obedient child will eventually know the secrets.

If no one had bothered to tell me about the storm I would never have known. I was there but was just a baby. Daddy didn't tell me. It was one of the secrets he kept but I heard him telling somebody else. Just as sure as Daddy knew I'd discern which was going to be my chosen child, in time, he knew I'd fill in the blanks about that storm.

One day as I sat quietly and waited for a tumultuous storm to pass, my thoughts, like a whirlwind went straight to Daddy's horse, Malachi and, I just declare, the truth came to me as clear as a bell. I discerned every bit of what I hadn't known. For the first time, I was positive that's the way it was going to happen with my chosen child. That's how clear it will be. The child may not be thinking about Malachi but whatever the thought, it will be just as revealing. I prayed the revelation wouldn't focus on Mama. The children loved her so.

Mama never gave a hint to the children that our lives had been anything but perfect when she spoke to them about us, Daddy and Malachi. She never mentioned Will Johnson and his children. She didn't speak of Roxie Robinson's sister, Rosella.

As tall as Daddy, Mama stood straighter than most women half her age. Her energy was unwavering. She brushed her striped, black and grey hair backwards into a neat bun that gracefully complemented her slender neck. The color of coffee gently sprinkled with cream, colored the flawless skin on her slender, pointed chinned face and made her high cheeks appear majestic. Skirts covering her ankles so stiffly starched and perfectly ironed didn't wrinkle even if the children hugged, tugged and wallowed on her all day long. Her voice, soothing and mellow didn't quiver like a lady her age and the expressions in her hands were deliberate and elegant. Every now and then when speaking to the children, a twinkle came out of the past and glistened over the film in her dull, aging eyes. A genuine sparkle was difficult to muster and a genuine will to continue to live was lacking. The only reason Mama stayed alive was because she was too afraid to let go.

FOUR

Mama told the children that Daddy and Malachi were two of the bravest, strongest, living things made by God. She described them as being alike, both tall and Malachi's coat shiny and healthy as Daddy's glowing skin. Malachi's tail was thick, black and curled on the end like strains of Daddy's hair. I used to brush Malachi's mane and tail. I'd run my hands through Daddy's curly hair trying to feel one them being different from the other. Both liked for me to do it.

That ole horse had been around since Daddy was a boy. I believe he knew things too, like the strange way he acted the morning of that storm. Daddy had a hard time making him move. No matter how much Daddy said "step" Malachi made two steps forward and four steps back, rearing and whining and snorting before finally, reluctantly stepping.

I know how Daddy must have felt. I'd be awfully disappointed if he started to act strange along with suddenly being disobedient the way Malachi did that day. Malachi refusing to follow Daddy's commands was like the sun refusing to rise.

Daddy kept speaking gently to Malachi. Would never have dared lay a forceful hand on any living thing, much less, something he loved. He quietly begged Malachi saying a storm was brewing and he was trying to beat it. There wasn't a cloud in the sky that morning but like other strange things he knew, there was something else about that sky that made Daddy worried. It was the same way he knew about my little brother, John David. Hmm.... it's too difficult for me to think about John David and the storm story at the same time. The stories are connected but it doesn't wear well with me to think about them together.

Malachi and Daddy made that trek into the town of Franklinton many Saturday mornings. We looked forward to them getting back, most times, bringing us more than what we needed. As we grew bigger, he let us tag along and choose anything we wanted. Mama complained that letting us do that was being wasteful but when he brought nice things home to her, she didn't complain. She'd brag to others about all the good he did for her and his children. If Daddy didn't find her blackberries, figs or strawberries plump enough in town he'd stop to pick them on the way home.

That morning, Daddy folded his croker sacks, gathered and neatly stacked his buckets and baskets in the wagon, doing all the usual things until Malachi resisted. This wasn't the first time Daddy left home knowing a storm was brewing. He and Malachi always made it back safely. This time things felt different.

I have a picture in my mind of Mama watching from the porch not making sense of what was happening with Malachi that day. She watched them move along until she was startled when in the middle of a nap shorter than usual, I woke up screaming letting out a shrill that Daddy told me he could hear way down the road. He said I was just two months old and the sound was so piercing to his ears, that he started to come back home. When my thoughts dwell on that day I imagine my soul and body with the same sensations that I must have felt that day.

Mama left the door just long enough to pick me up. She said I was still raising a ruckus as she carried me back to the porch to watch until

Daddy and Malachi were out of sight. Anxiety made her body tense as she rocked and sang trying to pacify me:

"O the beautiful garden, the garden of prayer

O the beautiful garden of prayer

And my Savior awaits as He opens the gates

To the beautiful garden of prayer."

Mama whispered, "Let the garden open to my prayers." The vibrations I get when I think or hear about that day make me feel so bad.

Mama saw me looking her straight in her eyes when I heard her tell the children that Malachi was Daddy's only friend. Not true. Everybody in Washington Parish, Louisiana admired, respected and loved John Ricks. Without that kind of reputation, she wouldn't have married him. Every time she wasn't telling the truth about something, she turned her eyes toward me. When she told them how Daddy knew things, she **was** telling the truth and that day, feeling a brewing storm without a cloud in the sky was the reason she was nervous and why Daddy was in a hurry.

Mama told the children that Daddy created things to last. He made that wagon of his as sturdy and as dependable as Malachi. I heard her whisper to herself, "It's too bad he didn't make himself." Gaps in her sentences left pauses long enough for the children to wonder what she was thinking. When she paused like that, she was reflecting on Daddy's words wanting to be sure the words remained stored safely somewhere inside her. I felt sorrow for her and nervous when she went off that way. One of these times, I thought, she may not be able to bring herself back.

She continued, "My heart was so heavy that morning, I thought it was going to burst wide open. I carried my baby, your mama, to the porch and watched until I couldn't see your grandfather and Malachi in front of that thick cloud of dust being kicked up.

While Mama was telling her ever-changing version, I was thinking about the way all the other things happened like how nobody really knew when my daddy came to Louisiana. His arrival in Franklinton was as mysterious as he was. He told how he was actually heading further south to New Orleans but had grown too tired and weary when he came upon Franklinton. Said he didn't draw attention to himself on purpose. Trusting others didn't come easy after all the things he'd had to endure. There were lots of people moving place to place back then so there wasn't much questioning of strangers. Keeping ones eyes and ears wide open could teach more.

People in Franklinton thought they should be able to trust a man who could honestly figure up in his head how much he owed at the commissary faster than anyone did it with a pencil. At the lumber yard, measurements made with just his eyes were close to accurate. He'd been well trained in politeness and good manners. The people of Washington Parish slowly began to take notice. Some thought there was an aura hovering over him. They said he must have been Creole because of his light skin and his head full of not straight and not kinky hair. Some said looking to be almost six feet tall, he could have come from the Cherokee tribe. They said only hard work could build a body like the well-developed muscles budging in his shirt. Nobody was sure about any of that but what the people of Washington Parish saw was an honest, soft speaking stranger with the bounce of a spring in his walk.

Other men took advantage of the young man who was full of energy and considered smarter than the others. Daddy was hired and soon worked to supervise others. His job was to supervise the chipping of the turpentine trees and to make sure the quart containers were adequately filled with the viscous, brownish, yellow, smelly fluid that flowed out. I remember how Daddy's description gave me the first smell that ever lingered in my memory.

Mama loves to tell about how women for miles around with their eyes on Daddy wanted him for their daughters. Too bad, because Washington Parish's most eligible bachelor didn't socialize. Daddy was polite when he'd greet people but seldom engaged in lengthy conversations. Said he was too busy making himself comfortable, building his house and keeping a protective shield between himself and everybody else. That was, until one day he recognized a sight his eyes easily focused on.

At the commissary one day, Daddy found himself staring from behind a stack of wood. His concentration was so intense that he didn't notice Grandpa Frank and Grandma Caroline watching him gaze at their daughter. He wasn't the only one gazing. Mama was surreptitiously watching him watch her.

The man who seldom engaged in conversation, quietly asked his workers about Mama. Her name is Marjanna Cryer, they shared. She was too spoiled, one said, and no man was ever going to have enough of anything to give that would please her. Daddy laughed when he told us about that. Said he had enough of everything he needed, except the courage to approach Mama. Said whenever he saw Mama it made him uneasy. Told me he'd never felt that way about a woman and the pangs he was experiencing had to have been love. Said the feeling scared him. That's one of only a very few times I ever heard Daddy speak of being scared. One other time had to do with the day of the storm and another time I actually saw real fear in him, but that's another story.

Before Daddy met Mama, I'll bet he must have been awfully lonely. He had to have missed his sisters, Daphne and Adeline. He'd never been away from them in South Carolina until he came to Louisiana. He missed his mother, Clyde a lot. His father David Sr. and brother David Jr. must have frequently been on his mind. But now, at home in the evening, his thoughts were about Mama. What he couldn't have known was Grandpa Frank Cryer was thinking about him and had a trick up his sleeve.

One Saturday Daddy watched Mama and Grandma Caroline leaving the commissary with their arms loaded with packages. Grandpa Frank was pushing a wheelbarrow that over-flowed with even more stuff. Daddy listened at their footsteps marching across the wooden floor and of the three, stepping sounds, he distinguished the sound of Mama's feet from the others. He was looking in Mama's face that he said was more beautiful each time he saw her.

By the time Daddy eased to the front of the store to watch them from the window, the Cryers' packages were loaded. Grandpa Frank was bending, looking at his wagon wheel. Concerned about the frown Grandpa had on his face, Daddy forgot about being nervous. He rushed outside and right up to the wagon.

"Trouble with your wagon, sir?"

Grandpa Frank told Daddy, "The pin is out of the wagon tongue."

Before Daddy said hello to Mama and Grandma Caroline he and Grandpa started working on the tongue. Grandpa took advantage of the moments to ask Daddy a thousand questions. Did he go to church? Where did he live? Who lived with him? Why wasn't a smart young man like him already married? As they worked, Grandpa asked, and Daddy answered. Daddy's answers must have satisfied Grandpa.

It was only after the task was complete, a task that either man could easily have done alone, that Grandpa got around to inviting John Ricks to their house for Sunday dinner. The invitation excited Daddy so much, he started sweating. Wiping his brow, he pretended he was warm from the work he did on the wagon tongue. Their efforts to get the pin in place were equal but Grandpa Frank wasn't sweating. Mama said Daddy's ears turned red from embarrassment.

Daddy was too excited to notice the pin had been unbent or unbroken. Grandpa had removed the pin on purpose.

Grandpa gave Daddy directions to their place that was just on the other side of Chavis Creek.

"Just ask anybody. Everybody knows where we live."

"Thank you. See you in church and after church too!"

Daddy said he was so taken aback. He couldn't think of anything else to say. All he could think to do was to look over at Grandma Caroline and Mama. He wasn't so surprised that he didn't notice Mama's smitten expression which pleased him.

Daddy said he wanted to touch Mama's arm to help her climb aboard but said Grandpa deliberately moved to stand between the two of them. It was a cagey wink from Grandpa's eye at Grandma as he reached for Mama's arm to help her on the wagon before he reached to help Grandma.

Daddy polished his shoes Saturday night and again when he got up Sunday morning. He combed his hair three different ways before he was satisfied. The Cryers were going to see him for the first time, in a long time, if ever, without a hat. The doors to the church were still locked because he got there too early. He felt the service lasted too long or his patience with God that day was too short. Following Grandpa's wagon to their house even seemed to be too slow. He couldn't wait to know more about Mama.

Besides having a beautiful daughter, Daddy said the next thing he liked was that those Cryers could really cook. Said he hadn't had a meal that good since he left South Carolina. He couldn't help but take more than one helping of everything. Grandpa continued to ask questions as Marjanna listened, barely touching her food.

Looking at Grandpa when he spoke but actually giving the information to Mama, he blurted spontaneously, "I'm building me a house on the hill that's just as you pass Monroe Blackburn's place."

Remembering what others had warned about Marjanna, he was sending her a message that he had most of what he needed and all he didn't have that she wanted, he was capable of getting.

Grandma Caroline listened intently and remained cautious. She was quite aware of John Rick's reluctance to be precise about leaving South Carolina and coming to Louisiana but resigned herself to know that her daughter's choices must be her own.

After dinner Mama and Daddy walked down by Chavis Creek spending the rest of the afternoon talking. Mama said it was refreshing to converse with a man who spoke correct English along with having good manners. Daddy told her his mother, brother and sisters' names. Mama talked about her brothers Stewart and Oliver and her sisters Martha and Ida. After that day, Mama and Daddy walked together to the creek every other Sunday. When Grandpa fully approved of John Ricks, Daddy and Malachi started bringing Mama to town on Saturdays.

The shade and smell of pine trees, the plush, grass carpet, the stillness in sparkling, crystal clear, blue water, the private places beneath wild oaks, a lonely lady with large, hopeful eyes and a lonely, displaced, young man every unmarried woman in the parish wanted was the perfect setting down by Chavis Creek for a courtship to blossom. Daddy and Mama's lasted just long enough for Grandma and Grandpa to consider the amount of time to be decent. The day they jumped the broom at Crystal Springs A.M.E. Church was the kind of day that had never been seen at that church. Mama likes to think there has never been another wedding better than hers since. She was proud to know that to have married the most desired man around was her greatest accomplishment. At least I can be grateful to her for giving us Daddy.

FIVE

An old saying is that the second baby comes in nine months. The first one might come anytime. Daddy gave Mama all the things she wanted and all the babies she could have. There hadn't been so much talk in Franklinton since a red-headed drifter passed through town leaving abandoned, mothers with fatherless, red-headed babies behind.

My brother Willie's birth, Daddy said, had skeptics counting months on their fingers making sure it was nine. Eleven months later came my brother Carl. Then one hot, June day, 1907, I, their third child and first girl was born. They named me Claudie. My brothers called me Sister.

Mama said Daddy doted over me so much it made her jealous. He wanted to hold me most of the time he was home despite Grandma Caroline's protests. They said he studied my face harder than he studied his Bible.

"Her face is like my sister Adeline. The rest of her is like my sister Daphne."

Grandma said he said all kinds of things although it was too soon to tell.

Mama and Grandma said Willie and Carl's cradles would have been just fine for me. Daddy wouldn't hear of it. Said he needed to make one especially for a girl. Pretty! He cut into the headboard carving the shape of a heart. Must have been a secret where he retrieved that lump of gold he also molded into a heart to fit perfectly in the opening of the cradle.

"That's the crown for my princess daughter's head."

Grandma fussed until he started again to spend more time at work. She didn't want the competition. He said it was always going to be hard for him to leave me.

Grandma Caroline did her share of doting, sewing fast to have me new things to wear almost everyday along with frilly bed linens, gowns and caps. Grandma Caroline said we were coming so fast, Mama needed all the help she could get. The women of Franklinton came to help Grandma and Mama because Mama had to stay in bed for six weeks. If a baby was born too fast those other ladies came and didn't leave until Grandma and Mama's sisters, Aunt Ida and Aunt Martha got there.

Mama didn't care whether Daddy went back to work or whether Grandma was making baby things. She was busy loving having the babies and mostly getting the attention that came with it. She didn't mind being in bed for six weeks and having everyone wait on her. Moving directly from the safe arms of Grandpa and Grandma into the loving care of John Ricks, she'd never had to be solely responsible for much of anything. Nobody knew what she might have been capable of doing by herself. Grandma and Grandpa didn't bother to mention to Daddy just how fickle Mama was. What they had wanted was to get her married and after she met Daddy, they hadn't needed to think much of her insecurities. She was now his responsibility.

SIX

Mama and I didn't touch each other much with loving feelings long before we came to Memphis. She received the genuine, loving touches she longed for from my children. The day of the storm she was holding me close to her, rocking and rocking and rocking. When I begin to remember how it was when she touched me with love, I'd stroke my hand across my cheek recalling how she'd take my hand and rub it across her soft, warm face while I nursed her breast. But that day, preoccupied with thoughts of Malachi and Daddy, she didn't know when I fell asleep. A veil of darkness covering the room jolted her. I woke up when I felt her body jump.

Rolling, black clouds pushing other billowing masses making their way across the sky put her in the same mood as the fiercely, approaching weather. She retrieved her wash outside as high winds were sweeping brush and cinders around in the field. In her thoughts, she was relieved that the storm wasn't blowing toward the direction Daddy was coming. Her typically, panicky irrationalizing thought was that it might push him backwards and if the ferocious weather were coming toward the house, maybe it could bring him home faster. Said she wanted to see Daddy coming so bad, she imagined the road started to move toward her instead of in the direction that had taken him away. She made Willie and Carl sit closer to her rocking chair as she squeezed the chair arms so tight her hands became numb and blue. She let go when she heard me stirring just long enough to rock the cradle.

Ooooooo! She said the wind gave off the sound of a hundred locomotives with just as many whistles. The house was shaking. A sky that dark in the middle of the day with my daddy nowhere in sight made Mama's body cringe causing mine to do the same thing.

Mama spent her life brooding or worrying about one absurd thing or another. Her thoughts drifted to, *what if he stopped at some other woman's house to get out of the storm and she seduced him? What if his proud air is mistaken for arrogance and offends the wrong white man or even a colored man? He's not arrogant. He just looks proud that way.*

A loud cracking sound like a tree crashing right through the roof shattered Mama's unsettling thoughts. She raised her eyes just in time to see the chimney fall, grazing the side of Willie's head before landing on his leg trapping him in place. The screaming duet of Willie and Carl was no match for Mama's holler. She was jumping up and down, turning around and around yelling "HELP! HELP! HELP!". She crotched in a corner after becoming dizzy from that whirling frenzy and buried her face in her hands. Carl was so afraid, he tried to hold on to the tail of her skirt, but she pushed him away making him topple. He became more afraid of her than he was of the storm. He crawled over to get closer to Willie. The tempest raged on.

With her face buried in her hands and her eyes closed, Mama didn't see the pain in Willie's face and the fear in Carl's eyes. Her incessant sobbing didn't allow her to hear the bolt on the door splitting its frame blowing wide open slamming against the wall. She didn't see my cradle looking as light as a feather float above the floor, whirling and dancing to the rhythm of the wind until it was sucked right out of the door.

Bent branches and uprooted trees lay sprawled across the road in Daddy's path. Remnants of houses and other debris floated in rapidly rising water already at the top of Daddy's boots and he wasn't half-way home. Daylight faded into mid-day darkness as Daddy jumped logs and waded in newly made streams trying to stay on a path leading him home. He said there was little left that he recognized. For the first time in his life he'd have to go on without Malachi.

Daddy found Mama outside, tangled in a holly bush, sobbing hysterically, scratched and bruised but safe. He kissed her as he gently lifted her from the twisted brush.

"Where are the children, Marjanna?"

Still uncontrollably sobbing she grasped Daddy's shirt with one hand while pointing toward what was left of their house with the other. His wet shirt slipped from her grip.

Willie was in shock from the pain of that heavy, brick chimney on his leg. My big strong daddy lifted that chimney while at the same time his eyes took pictures of everything else. Debris covered every spot, even the balled-up mass that turned out to be Carl. Daddy didn't languish one second over seeing evidence of his hard labor reduced to shreds. Anguish swelled on his insides when he saw one of his sons in pain, bleeding from his head, the other one scared out of his wits and their mother nowhere near to comfort them. The torment became more profound when he didn't see the crib.

A splintered piece of wood and a ripped cloth was the best he could do to make a splint for Willie's leg. Daddy's mere presence calmed Carl and made him stand straight up just to show Daddy how brave he was. Daddy picked him up, brushed debris from his hair, sitting him close to Willie as his wandering eyes kept searching for me.

Rushing, rolling, rising water along with continual, roaring, raging wind was nerve-wrecking. Daddy said he was scared.

"God, I found two of my children and my wife. Please don't let my other child be under the water."

Above all that noise, Daddy thought he heard laughing. He moved as swiftly as he could through the dimness toward the sound. Through the dim light of dusk, he saw the reflections of a shiny gold heart.

"Bless my soul", he used to say, "There she was, strongly holding her head barely above water, cooing, laughing out loud, using that cradle like it was a boat and her frilly pink top tangled like an anchor."

Daddy said he untangled me from that twisted wood, his hands feeling like a sturdy shield. He held me close to his rain-soaked breast and cried.

He said looking through his tears and my laughing eyes, he searched his heart and recognized a secret. That was the day he was sure I was his chosen child. He said throughout my life, I was destined to emerge unscathed from life's inevitable storms and keep my head above raging, dangerous water. After the first time I heard the story told, it would be the first time I noticed how knowing began to grow clearer in me.

At the end of Mama's telling the storm story, the children were so mesmerized they didn't seem to be able to move right away. I saw their stomachs rising and falling without hearing the deep breaths flow from their nostrils. One of them asked Mama to show them with her hands how little I was. I didn't hear Mama answer. Her eyes had already drifted up to a corner of the room. I moved toward her and stayed close while she disappeared into a deep dark memory, only she and God knows where.

SEVEN

At first, some of the people in Franklinton didn't know how to figure Daddy and he wasn't willing to help them. He, just as they did, watched and listened. He'd help in fulfilling any need for anyone if he could and was capable of doing most anything, but it didn't mean he wanted to be their friend. Some never realized that he didn't. Monroe Blackburn knew the difference but never stopped trying to be Daddy's friend. Daddy wasn't obliging. If friends were to be chosen, Daddy was determined he'd be the one doing the choosing. Daddy saw Monroe as he was. He was a white man and my daddy believed all white men believed in the same thing. Daddy's family's experiences in South Carolina let him understand what white men stood for.

Daddy kept a safe distance between our closest neighbors, but Monroe Blackburn's wife, Vee and Mama were not so standoffish. The two women became friends when both couples were still newly-weds. Twice they were both pregnant at the same time. Vee had a set of twins, a boy and a girl, Starcie and Steven born at the same time Mama had Carl. Her second set of twins, Walter and William, were born in 1907, the year I was born. After two sets of twins, Vee didn't have more children, but Mama's babies kept coming.

Mama and Vee looked out for each other while taking care of their houses, children and husbands. They sewed us girls dresses just alike. Daddy didn't like it at first but that didn't stop the Ricks and Blackburn children from racing, fishing, swimming, rolling in mud, making mud pies together. Mama and Vee shared recipes and all kinds of secrets. They talked all the time about that terrible storm of 1907. No matter what the topic of their conversation, that storm always crept in. They dissected that storm day and anything else that happened around it both, before and after.

One day I heard Mama telling Vee something about what happened to Uncle David in South Carolina. At the time, I couldn't understand how that terrible storm had anything to do with South Carolina and Uncle David. They even talked about how Daddy and Monroe helped everybody else but not each other.

"Vee, I'm sorry for John's refusing to accept Monroe's help. Monroe doesn't deserve to be treated that way."

"John can't help it, Marjanna. He has enough good reasons to feel the way he does."

"It's too embarrassing. I begged him to let Monroe help rebuild our house. Told him y'all were good people and how sincere Monroe is when he offers his help. John said I wouldn't know sincerity if it stepped in front of me and slapped me down. I'm always talking about how cute and smart your children are. He said your children aren't as cute or as smart as ours. Said you didn't have anything better than what I have and the reason you had twins twice was because you were too lazy to have them one at a time."

Vee wasn't offended. They both laughed.

"John said my parents sheltered me while reminding me of what happened to his South Carolina family. I often reminded him of what David said about building a shell around his mind and closing his heart to the others. He told me how David warned him about white people too. He wouldn't believe me when I told him you and Monroe weren't the kind of white people like those ole Klansman-like folks in South Carolina. He said he owed white people an honest day's work for an honest day's pay but that wasn't all white people owed him. Said they couldn't give him back the lives of his brother and father that they took. Said white people could never make up to him the pain he felt missing his mother and sisters, knowing he could never return to see them again. I told John that he shouldn't blame you all and asked that he should, at least, be polite to Monroe. He grew weary of my talking about it and told me he was going to try. He admitted that the hard shell that was growing tighter around his heart was uncomfortable, felt unnatural and eventually might squeeze him to death."

Mama reminded Vee how Monroe had extended his hand more than once and Daddy refused to accept.

"I asked him to at least be polite to Monroe. He said he'd think about it only because he didn't want his children to imitate his behavior."

Daddy didn't like the ladies' close friendship at first, but his ice-coldness began to thaw once he could see that any attempt to make changes would be futile. He was delighted to see the Ricks children and the Blackburn children racing, swimming, fishing, climbing trees, wallowing in mud, making mud pies and everything else together except going to school or church.

Mama and Vee spoke about how Franklinton was slow to recover from the loss of so many turpentine trees. Before the storm, turpentine was already becoming less of a demand than the lucrative business of selling those sturdy pine trees to railroad people. They talked about how fast the railroad industry was taking over and how it needed pine timber for cordwood.

I missed the pungent smell of turpentine on Daddy after he stopped being around the chipping of the trees but was glad he could spend more time at home. Mama was having babies so fast, we were outgrowing our house, so Daddy started to build us a brand new one. He told Mama he had to be sure, from then on, he had done his very best to make us as safe as could be. Seems like Daddy was always upgrading, repairing or reinforcing many things.

A sun-burned giant, Monroe Blackburn covered his curly, brown hair with different colored as well as stripped bibbed caps pulled down close to large, grey eyes that glistened when he faced the sun. He strode over and worked his land with the same confidence, pride and gestures of love as Daddy. For my daddy to ignore his friendship, there must gave been a good reason. I grew to know Monroe meant well.

Daddy didn't want Monroe Blackburn noseying around in our business, yet he was being nosey himself. Every chance he got he'd watch Monroe out of the corner of his eye. He couldn't yet trust him especially after one day Mama told Vee how John saw Monroe talking to the census man, pointing to our house. Both of those men were white, so it didn't feel right to watch them, knowing Monroe was speaking about us. He suddenly didn't think we were safe.

"Marjanna, the man was trying to ask questions about your family. Monroe only answered questions about us. Told the census man John could speak for himself."

"Then, why was Monroe pointing at our house?"

"The man asked where did the Rickes live."

When Daddy spoke to the man, he understood that just as other white people, the census man took for granted, Negroes were not capable of answering for themselves.

"Monroe told the man that John was more than capable of speaking for himself."

When Daddy spoke to the man, he could clearly see on the census list beneath Willie and Carl's names was my name listed as ***Typinia-female-age3-father, John-mother, Marjanna.***

John said, "Now who in the world would name their child Typinia. What kind of name is that?"

He thought Monroe had done it.

"Monroe knows all of your children's names, Marjanna, especially Sister. He adores her and knows her name is Claudie"

"Don't ever let John hear you say that. He thinks he's the only man who's suppose to adore her."

They laughed again.

Sometimes Mama and Vee talked, cooked and ate all day long. I didn't understand how they stayed so slim. I guess it was because they were always busy with us and their house work. I watched Vee listening intently to Mama. She at times nervously twisted a lock of her curly, blonde hair, her large green eyes peering into Mama's. That's when I could tell the conversation was serious. I wanted to understand everything they talked about but when they engaged in what they called "grown folks talk", they made us leave them alone. I'd eavesdrop anyway so when I got older, I could ask Daddy what all of it meant, especially the part about what happened to Uncle David. I had to wait a while before I asked so I'd just keep on listening.

"John said the census taker is white as cotton with an attitude of the same color. Said you all are white folks and he needs to keep his distance."

Vee looked concerned.

"But Monroe told that man how wrong he was for making up a name for Sister. Monroe cursed at that man when the man said, "It don't make no difference what her name is. Niggers' names don't mean nothing to us white folks. They wouldn't have any names anyway if it wasn't for us white folks."

When I heard Vee say that I almost had a nosebleed. Daddy never told us white people hated us so much. I thought everybody loved us like Mama, Daddy, Grandma Caroline and Grandpa Frank, Aunt Martha, Aunt Ida, Uncle Stewart and Uncle Oliver. Then I began to wonder how the Blackburn twins, Starcie and Steven and Walter and William felt about us. I'd never thought of their being any color until then when I noticed their skin was suddenly, too white. But they were my friends. I couldn't imagine their whiteness as the same kind Vee and Mama were talking about. They must have been speaking about a different kind of white. When I really looked at them, they were the same kind of white as their father who had the same whiteness as the census man and Monroe. It was the same kind Daddy didn't like. My feelings were identical to my Daddy's. He wasn't feeling hatred. Just wrestling with turmoil. I wanted not to feel any different than I'd always felt about the Blackburns. Something inside of me wouldn't let me change, anyway.

Daddy corrected the man about my name. The man cursed at my daddy. Mama ran from the porch begging Daddy to leave well enough alone. Willie and Carl started screaming too. I didn't scream. I knew my daddy could handle that scroungy looking man. If Id known any better, I would have cried AND screamed. It was before I grew to know that Negro men could be hung for talking back to white men. When Daddy turned to look at Willie and Carl, Mama said that gave him pause enough to be quiet and not hit the man, but Mama said the turmoil of his distrust of white skin was raging. Bitterness rose in Daddy like bread dough full of yeast. He didn't trust any white man. He was reminded again that Monroe and Vee Blackburn were as white as that census man.

Daddy never said Mama couldn't be friends with Vee nor did we see his disapproval of us and the Blackburn children playing together but us having as little contact as necessary with white folks would have been just fine with him.

Monroe and Vee were very aware of other Louisiana parishes where colored and white people had absolutely nothing to do with each other. Some places didn't even allow Negroes to pass through their towns. Monroe knew bad white people did bad things to Negroes and he didn't agree. He wanted to be a friend to a decent man like John Ricks, not a friend to one like the census man just because he was white. He understood Daddy's resistance to his friendly gestures but was hopeful that in time Daddy would be able to know his heart was filled with sincerity. He wished Daddy's smart eyes would be able to see he hadn't been tarnished with prejudices and hate.

EIGHT

Daddy sometimes anguished over the day of that 1907 storm and how with one stronger, gigantic burst of wind the life could have been snatched right out of all of us. He wrestled with the thought of how if my neck hadn't been strong enough to hold my little head above water, that with just one more drop of rain, I could have drowned. Surely, Mama loved us all, he thought, but why was she outside when Carl was trembling with fear. All he needed was a reassuring hug. And Willie, his leg trapped under chimney bricks, didn't see Mama even attempt to release his leg or did she even notice his pain and his bleeding head. I still wonder if she even tried to find me and my cradle.

Daddy's pain came from blaming himself for everything. Said he should have made the house more substantial. Said he'd never trust being so far from home too long without us, again. From then on, wherever he went, all of us went. If Mama was carrying a child and her stomach was too big, she wanted to be dropped off at the Blackburn house while the rest of us tagged along. His thoughts had him already carrying around enough weight without his having to be concerned about making friends with Monroe and Vee Blackburn.

I didn't care if Mama didn't come with us sometime. Daddy let us act more grown up when she stayed at home. She said girls didn't need to know how to choose quality seeds and to spot signs of rodents and bugs on flour sacks. Said only boys should know those kinds of things but Daddy taught us all the same especially if Mama wasn't there. All of us learned to measure with our eyes; to count our money and not be cheated and how to negotiate to get the most for our pennies. He taught us to be good listeners while we searched for signs of sincerity in voices. We learned how to be cordial without being too friendly and to be leery of certain people. He loved to teach us and I noticed, if he kept busy with us when we were around others, he didn't have time for anybody else.

We liked some of the people we met and most of them acted like they liked us. There was one lady, Miss Rozella, who was Roxie Bright's sister, who acted as if she wished she didn't have to see us. For a long time, I had to wonder about her reason. She'd roll her eyes and turn her big nose up like she could smell something nasty when she'd see us. Daddy never let his eyes meet hers and tried to stay on the opposite side of the store when she came in. I'd tell Mama how Miss Rozella didn't like us. Mama said it was my imagination.

While in town, the only thing Daddy didn't let me do was go with my brothers to explore the town. I wanted to find out if they were telling me the truth about their experiences. On our way home they told us fascinating tales about where they'd been and what they had seen. They told about watching men give their money away shooting dice. Daddy said the boys shouldn't be caught hanging around those men. He'd gently scold them for mischief and was generous with his praise and lessons when they pleased him.

Daddy took advantage of every opportunity to teach us lessons. At home, he read us Bible verses. Some of them he read so often we couldn't help but know them by heart. He always read, 'Honor thy father and thy mother'. 'Forgive those who trespass against you', was another. He'd make us repeat after him, 'Depart from evil and do good. Seek peace and know it'. Then, there were his own words, "Deafen your ears and close your mind and heart to everything except the voice that speaks inside yourself. Everything under the sun has a season. Wait for the right season before you act. Do not worship anything except what's made by God and everything else in our lives will find their rightful place."

The lessons in the stories Daddy told us about Roundsboro, South Carolina always turned out to be pleasant. He boasted about the courage of his father, David Ricks, Sr. He smiled but his eyes looked sad when he spoke of our Uncle David, Jr.'s strength and courage and how the roar of his laugh was mesmerizing. When he talked about his sisters, Daphne and Adeline he made it seem that they were the purist women in the world besides us and Mama. After my sister Clyde was born, he compared her sweetness to his mother whose name was Clyde and said my sister could wear the name with honor.

While in town, when Willie and Carl were disobedient, most of the time it didn't bother Daddy. There were times when they'd be late getting back to meet us. Daddy said boys have to be free to explore what all is in the world. I wanted to know the reason girls couldn't know too. Daddy said I already knew more. I thought he was just trying to make me feel better.

One day, Willie and Carl's freedom to explore what was in the world lasted too long. It sent Daddy reeling. He grew impatient when he saw the wind rising high enough to bend tree limbs. He and I watched restless clouds merge into one gigantic, dark blob. With his thumbs twiddling, he paced back and forth. I paced with him making three steps to his one, watching as he studied the unstable sky. As we watched Willie and Carl run toward the wagon, Daddy said he was deciding whether to let the approaching storm blow over before we started home. When he thought about Mama being by herself, he quickly dismissed the thought of waiting. Daddy motioned toward the wagon for us to hurry and get in before coaxing Malachi into a steady trot. Willie and Carl sensed his pensiveness and knew this wasn't the time for sharing their adventures of a fabulous tale.

Raindrops the size of grapes danced on and around the wagon splattering one into the other until we were surrounded by a blowing shower. It was the kind of soft, quiet rain Daddy said was created just for children. If we'd been at home they would have allowed us to play outside in it. Even while riding on the wagon I would have enjoyed getting wet that day if Daddy hadn't looked so worried.

The weather didn't turn out nearly as threatening as the expression on Daddy's face. We made it home drenched, windblown and safe.

Willie and Carl jumped out, running in the left-over drizzle, whispering secrets to each other they didn't share on the way home. They stopped to splash around in a mud puddle as Daddy started to unload the wagon. Mama was going to have a few words of her own if they tracked mud in the house.

Carl ran in the house first. Before Willie could get his muddy feet in the door, Carl bumped past him saying, "There's nobody in there."

I ran inside past both of them to see if Carl was telling the truth. We'd never had an empty house unless all of us were away together. I felt the emptiness inside the house but felt peace inside of me. In time I grew to know why.

Daddy dropped the sack of sugar, taking one giant step to the porch and another inside the door. He did a slow run through the rest of the house noting the feel of its emptiness. Everything in the house seemed to be in its rightful place.

"Marjanna! Marjanna!

He walked out the back, down toward the well finding no sign of Mama anywhere. Nothing was making any sense.

"What's going on here?"

At the edge of the porch he kept calling and calling only to be answered by echoes bouncing and circling around us. Just as he turned to call from a different direction we were startled by heavy, muddy, mushy steps from somebody's big shoes. He recognized Monroe Blackburn's voice before discerning who the shadowy, towering figure was that was moving toward us beneath the remaining dreary skies.

When Monroe got close enough for Daddy to look in his face, his gut-wrenching past flashed before him and irrationally intertwined with the present. Memories from South Carolina, of his sister, Daphne, running to bring him dreadful news was creating the delusion. From a flash in the glowing streaks of the setting sunlight that came flickering on the edge of a heavy cloud, Daddy said he saw Monroe Blackburn's face as the face of Daphne. He searched Monroe's face looking for anguish. There wasn't any. Eyes that were supposed to show concern, the same as had been in Daphne's eyes, were wide and full of anticipation. Hands from this figure weren't waving hysterically as Daphne's had been. One steadied at his side. The other was extended toward Daddy.

"John if you're looking for Marjanna, she's at our house. We came for her when the weather turned nasty. Vee said she should stay with us until you got back."

Daddy didn't answer. The two men just stood there face to face, one black, one white, one reluctant and suspicious, the other sincere and hopeful.

"Come on John. What is it with you?"

Monroe kept his hand extended toward Daddy, refusing to pull it back. Nothing on Daddy's body moved except his roaming, gazing eyes.

"John, don't you want to see your new boy?"

Daddy's eyes danced back and forth from one of Monroe's eyes to the other.

What in the world did he say? Marjanna couldn't have had the baby. It isn't time. I've been near when each of my children was born and will do the same with this one. But what is this about? This man is a stranger to me and a white stranger at that, standing before me talking to me about precious things.

Daddy acted like he didn't want to hear another word from Monroe. He scooped me up in his arms and started running toward the Blackburn house.

"Come on Willie! Come on Carl!"

For the first time in my life I prayed for a miracle and knew a miracle was getting ready to happen.

Daddy was running so fast, if Vee hadn't opened the door and stepped aside, Daddy would have crashed right through it and smashed her to pieces.

He stared at Mama momentarily before he lifted my little brother out of Mama's arms.

"Meet Aaron", Mama said softly with a look of concern, unsure of what was going to happen next. I couldn't wait to see.

When Daddy leaned over and kissed Mama, even I could feel something turning him loose. He turned to acknowledge his captive audience. Willie, Carl, Walter, William, Starcie, Steven, Monroe, Vee and me all watched in silence.

With Aaron nestled securely in one arm, Daddy reached out with the other toward Monroe.

"Thank you, Monroe! Thank you, Vee! Thank both of you for taking care of my wife and son."

With a tight grip on Daddy's hand, Monroe replied, Anytime, John."

Innocent children connected and collectively happy in a moment that had been created to always be remembered, is a moment to behold. As for me, my prayer had been answered. A miracle had happened and then I understood the peace I had felt.

From that day on, the Ricks children got a chance to live and laugh and play without feeling that something was wrong. The Blackburn children were the only real friends we'd ever known.

Until Mama was strong enough to go home, Vee took care of everybody. Daddy and Monroe stayed together at our house working between the two houses. They had lots of catching up to do.

Daddy stopped being concerned about leaving home without us. We were never alone. Monroe was always looking out for us and Daddy looked out for Vee and their children if Monroe was away.

I knew Daddy was sorry for the way he'd acted toward Monroe and glad Monroe persisted in pursuing a friendship. Daddy said he came close to missing out on something genuine. Getting to know each other better each day, working side by side, even allowed them to speak to each other in ways nobody else understood.

"Mr. Blackburn."

"Yes, Mr. Ricks."

"When you talk, don't speak to me in that tone. You're not my boss. Have you considered looking at either of us, lately?" You're about as dark as I am."

Seeing them together, their genuine laughter blending in harmony, created the most beautiful melody.

I knew this friendship was right. Daddy did too. As the friendship grew, his attitude toward many things changed. He didn't hate all white people anymore like his brother David went to his grave doing. There were other things he'd been taught by Uncle David that made him feel he could breathe freely without choking. The shell that was crushing his heart slowly dissolved. It had been a rigid shell like the one that had choked Uncle David to death.

NINE

I go to my windows to call forth memories, both wretched and endearing. The directions I have taken in life gave me no choices. It depended on how brazen the forces were in my heart. Facing south helps me to purge pain while I hold tightly to pleasures. Turning north, I live and re-live my future. The road west was destined to be taken by my brothers and sisters. When I look in my mirror, I see somebody I love that I've never met. There's someone enchanting in my coal-black braid I comb and plait everyday. My braid looks like the one in our treasure box. Also, there's something captivating about the gold locket Daddy gave me that came from that same treasure box.

At my windows, I can hear the chirping sounds of crickets coming from the east, all the way from a place called Roundsboro, South Carolina where the Ricks family secret is hidden. I heard about the secret in the lessons Daddy taught us. Now, my children hear them in the lessons I pass on to them. Just as I did, the children will search for understanding like the knowledge of things I needed to know about why I feel pain when I smell sawdust and pleasure when the smell of turpentine and tobacco invade my nose. I needed to know why blue to me is reverent. I needed to know the reason I hated the sound of those crickets but love the sight in the mirror of things like my braid that makes me myself. My heart cries out with a longing to go to a place I've never been and to know somebody I've never seen except in me.

My special place is at my windows. Daddy had a place in the woods that was to him like my windows are to me. After the storm he cut up the damaged trees for firewood. In a particularly, chosen place, he smoothed a stump creating a comfortable place to sit and think. He loved the smell of bark and wildflowers. He spoke to squirrels, deer, and raccoons. He felt right at home when surrounded by natural things and didn't like to see them tarnished. This place on a stump in the woods was his very private domain.

One day while I was looking for sea grass to make hair for Thelma's doll, I came upon Daddy in his sacred place. That stump and all that surrounded it was his personal sanctuary but that day it was different. He shared his sacred place with Monroe Blackburn. Monroe sat on the ground looking up at Daddy as he listened.

I eased close enough to hear Daddy tell Monroe how he couldn't get over the feelings he had the morning of the 1907 storm. Said he thought a lot about the unusual way Malachi had acted and the pleading he'd heard in my cry. He told Monroe how that day made him remember a night in South Carolina when he'd had the same uneasy feelings. Said he was sure, because of those feelings, he may have been possessed with a gift but sometimes, he thought, it could also be a curse.

"Monroe, I prayed for understanding and found it."

Daddy recited verses from the Bible Daphne and Adeline had taught him. Said he was glad they insisted he learn them by heart.

I felt compelled to eaves drop and stayed hidden behind a tree to listen.

He said, "My sister Daphne was as beautiful as any creature God created. She was as tall as I but slim as a switch. I used to tease her with her thick, black braid that hung down her back to her waist. Man, she'd let out the most joyful sounding laugh when I'd grab that braid and hit her in the face with it. No matter how much I teased, it never annoyed her. I'd take the scissors and threaten to cut off that braid. She pretended she believed I was serious."

'Please John, don't cut off my braid. That's my glory. You wouldn't want me to lose my glory, would you?'

"My folks were always talking about glory."

Daddy said, one day when he started thinking seriously about Daphne's glory, he thought, nobody had told him what a man's glory was. When he asked Daphne, she was serious when she answered.

She told him, 'A man's glory is shown in the fruits of his works, his honesty and his faith in God. But his glory shows mostly in his wife.'

"A wife? Not me!"

"Oh yes. Especially you. You have to be sure you chose the right lady."

"What about you and Adeline. Getting hitched is for women too. Y'all need to make yourselves somebody's glory."

"Don't you be concerned about me and Adeline. We have to make good choices too. When the right men show up, we'll know it and will welcome them. It's you we want to be sure about."

Adeline laughed. "I'm not in a hurry. I'll let Daphne go first and see how she likes it before I try it. Besides, John, when you and Daphne get married and leave, I'm going to be the one to stay here with Mother and David."

"My mother stopped, looking up from the task at hand the way she did when she was going to say something seriously important."

"Nobody's going to hide behind my skirt, Adeline. I can take care of myself, very well. Both of you know how to take care of yourselves and a man. Don't you? You shouldn't worry about John just yet. He still has plenty of time."

"That's right, Mother", I chimed in. I'm not going to get married. I'll be the one to stay here with you and David."

Daddy continued, "Monroe, we took for granted that David was the one never to be married. David did more listening than talking but when he spoke, my ears were well trained to pay attention."

"John, you don't have to worry about taking care of these ladies. A day is going to come when they'll have to take care of themselves', David warned. 'And you'll know when the time is right and you'll understand the things you're suppose to do. I'm proud of how well you've learned all you need to know."

"I didn't understand what my brother's words meant at the time and couldn't see how clearly my understanding of them was inevitable."

It was the kind of stifling, Louisiana day that was great for napping. Monroe didn't get sleepy. He focused his eyes right into Daddy's and listened intently. I watched and listened so long I was afraid Mama was going to send somebody looking for me. I sat frozen as I watched how full of love his words sounded when he spoke about his sisters.

"Adeline was the youngest of all of us. Monroe, I wish you could have seen her. Well, I wish you could have seen all of them."

"What about us taking a trip to see them? You never talk about it but Vee, the children and I would be thrilled to go with you all to see them."

"I can't go back and even if I could, you couldn't go with me."

"I can go wherever I want."

"You're not that dumb. Let me finish telling you."

"Adeline wasn't quite as tall as the rest of us but had more energy than the three of us together. She bounced delicately around that house almost never still. She cherished how she was free to do whatever she wanted. That girl loved to feel her hands in dirt, searching for clovers and making beautiful things grow. It was what she was born to do. She planted sweet potatoes and white potatoes. The fruit from her apricot trees were so perfectly orange you'd think she'd colored them with a paint brush. The tall stalks of corn had the sweetest, juiciest ears. My father told her how rare, precious and special she was. He said special people could make beautiful things grow. Everyday when she finished the work in her garden, she'd rake her hands through the clover patch until she found her four-leaf clover for the day. She always found one, too. The rest of us had to search a long time and most of the time didn't find one at all. Sometimes, I'd find her hiding in her garden, in deep thought, fondling a locket my daddy gave her one Christmas when she was about five years old. I knew when her hand was tight around it, she was missing him. She never took if off. You see, Monroe, our father left for work one day and never came back. Remembering all things he taught us, making things come alive and flourish was Adeline's way of trying to feel my father alive."

Monroe looked stunned but didn't speak.

"The day my father didn't come home my mother said she didn't know what happened, but she could feel he was dead. I believe Mother would have died too if her children hadn't been so young. Told us how she couldn't stand the thought of us losing both so she made up her mind to live until she was sure we could make it on our own. When we started growing up, looking more like young men, her hair turned rapidly gray. The deeper our voices got and as the hair grew thicker above our upper lips, the more she worried. Her mouth at times quivered as she talked to us when she was really studying the men we were becoming."

"You all act just like your father. You walk proud, talk proud and aren't afraid of anything", she said.

"I have to give David credit for some of the way I am. He stepped right in and took over where my father left off. David taught me to read and write, to measure with my eyes, to count and not to fear anything but God and evil. He showed me how to see the favorable signs of nature and the bad signals too. I learned to know what the other creatures of God were feeling and the meaning of their every motion. I sensed each time there was danger. In making sure I understood it all, David was also teaching me how to believe there was something else, special within me, I would, at the right time, come to know."

Monroe stood for just a moment hitting at and missing a bug before he took his seat again not appearing the least bit uncomfortable.

"Oooh, Monroe, I wish you could have seen him. He was a big man with a wide chest and sparkling grey eyes that matched the silver lining I always remember around his dark temples. When I did things well, he smiled a smile as wide and as happy as babies'. He made me think I pleased him most of the time. Even if I didn't please him his scolding was so gentle. David liked being alone a lot. Had a favorite Palmetto tree he used to sit and lean against always with his Bible, paper and pencil. When he wasn't reading, he was scribbling on that paper. He seemed happy all alone as if he was entertaining himself. When he laughed it rolled and rumbled like thunder through the woods. We could hear it all the way up to the house. He wanted to love everything. I'd see him listening to the rushing water swirling over rocks in a stream. He enjoyed the night, watching the stars and made wishes when they'd fall. Much love as David had for other things, he didn't feel the same way for white people He hated them."

Monroe dropped his head when Daddy said that. Daddy didn't stop talking.

"I wanted to go to work in the sawmill with David."

"No, John. Your place is right here taking care of what's ours."

"I said, but David I'm old enough."

"Yes, and you're strong enough too but somebody's got to stay here and that somebody is you."

"I argued with him but not too much."

"He told me", "The only time you can leave this place is when the time is just right and the time is not right yet. That sawmill isn't a place for a man looking as proud as you. That place kills a man's spirit. Stay here until it's time for change to come. You'll know when the time is right. Listen to what comes from the inside of you. Use what you know to do good. Those white men that work at the mill in the daytime also wear white sheets and ride at night. They'd kill me today if I'd give them half the chance."

"David was concerned because when men are afraid they eliminate what they fear. They were afraid of David but tried not too show it. My brother's back was striped like a zebra's after men at the sawmill held him down and beat him. The more David tried to fight back the harder they hit. Afterwards that foreman wore that whip tied to his belt like it was a trophy and as a warning to others. We were told that my father walked right up to that foreman, knocked him down, took that whip and came close to choking that white man to death with the very whip that had scarred my brother's back. Not surprisingly, we never saw my father again. But......!"

Daddy paused looking pensive. Monroe stayed quiet.

"That wasn't the end of it. It wasn't long before that foreman disappeared. They were suspicious of my Daddy, but men were always disappearing around that saw mill. Nobody put forth one bit of effort to find any of them. Probably wouldn't have done much good anyway. David told me by the time a body had been mangled and flattened it was unrecognizable at the other place of wherever it had been shipped.

After Daddy disappeared, David didn't let much come out of him and he didn't allow much to get on the inside of him either. He reminded me of how uncertain life was for men like us. He spoke of the night riders in white sheets with the eyes cut out. He told me everything to do if anything happened to him. Thinking of all that he taught me, I learned to love the things he loved and hate the things he hated."

"He told me", 'God doesn't take life before a man's time is up. God won't hang men in trees until they're dead or have them beaten or burned to death. Evil men killed our father. They almost killed me. I don't want the same thing to happen to you.'

I tried not to breathe because after hearing that, I had started taking such deep breaths I thought Daddy and Monroe could hear me breathing. At times, the only thing moving was Daddy's mouth. His words to me were muffling the evening sounds. Dusk along with those words made natural shadows in the woods appear spooky. Monroe looked glued to the ground and Daddy to his tree stump. Daddy was shining a light in the past, pushing the rest of his life forward. He continued.

"One night in South Carolina, I couldn't figure out why I couldn't sleep. The sounds of night had been my lullaby since my mother stopped singing me to sleep. Crickets weren't wailing. Owls didn't cry. There were no mating calls. The only thing I heard was anguish in the sounds of moaning. I heard a cry for mercy. The sound was someone in pain. I tipped to the window and heard sounds that were coming from David. He was sitting on the porch, rocking back and forth and side to side. He was grunting and praying. A feeling came over me that was so bad, it made me want to vomit. I was also led to know that I was not to interfere and I didn't, but I couldn't stop watching. My brother carried on that way until daylight came streaking through. I jumped into bed and didn't move, pretending to sleep when he came inside. Didn't want him to know I'd heard him and was too nervous to move anyway but I saw the kind of peace that had come over his face. I hadn't seen that look since before my father died.

David was always up early and tipped around to keep from disturbing us. He was quiet that morning too but did weird things. Instead of packing for work, he unpacked the things he usually carried in his work sack. I shut my eyes when he started toward me. He patted my head and paused to look down on me before he leaned over to kiss my forehead. He had never done that. Daddy did but not David."

Daddy paused again like he was re-living the moment all over again.

"Getting the rest of my day started was really hard. I thought it was because I was missing all that sleep I'd lost. I couldn't stop thinking about David's peculiar behavior. He had made painful sounds although he didn't act like his body was hurt. The cricket sounds that I didn't hear that night suddenly became too loud for it to be the middle of the day. The sun was in its right place but didn't seem to have its mid-day glare. The mule was having a hard time raising the ground even in the soft soil. I was going to retire that tired old mule at the end of the season anyway but that day I couldn't let him rest. Neither could I. I had to keep moving. I didn't stop even to eat but that didn't ease my nervousness. Too many strange things had gone on that I couldn't understand. I was just about to give up when I heard screaming. I looked toward the sound and saw Daphne in a frenzy running toward me, waving her hands up and down. I dropped the plow and ran to meet her."

"David is dead! David is dead!"

"We went limp in each others' arms."

"Cut him up like he was a piece of wood with that big sawing machine!"

"That's what she said, Monroe. Hearing the words and hearing Daphne's screams had me wishing I could turn time back to the day before yesterday. Thoughts of David's anguish the night before crowded my brain. His kiss on my forehead haunted me. My insides felt like they were being torn apart. I thought men with white skin don't have feelings or don't love anything. Blood from white hearts must run cold. All white men must die. For the first time in my life I didn't know what to do or how to do anything, I'd never been without David's strong shoulders to lean on. I'd never felt sadness without seeing David's newly born smile that melted my sadness or having his softly spoken words to encourage me or the gentle touch of a powerful hand to soothe me. I'd never had a problem that David didn't help me solve but there I was with a heavy burden and David was dead. Didn't know what I was going to do. Then, I began to understand David's suffering the night before and I believe David had understood it even more."

Monroe rubbed his chin just before he slapped his thigh.

"David's body was mutilated. There wasn't much left to bury. They wanted us to see him that way. One tough part for me was convincing my mother and sisters not to look.

I brushed David's Sunday suit before I folded it and slipped it into the coffin on which I did my finest work. I headed to his favorite spot that was by his Palmetto tree where he went to read, laugh, write and pray. With my shovel over my shoulder, my heart cried out for mercy. Until that day, I hadn't noticed the rocks that were stacked in the shape of a pyramid. I was careful not to disturb the flawlessness all around the place my brother loved. I handled each rock in the pyramid like precious chunks of gold moving them to make room for a grave. I dug and shoveled, dug and shoveled not realizing the sounds I was hearing were my own cries from the burial hole. Tiny quakes, I thought were coming from the ground were tremors from my own dented body. With each shovel of dirt and every thud after heart-breaking thud, a piece of my heart cracked. My strength was waning. I was blinded by tears. Suddenly when the hole was deep enough to throw dirt over my head, a stubborn stone became the biggest challenge. I yelled, how dare a stone! How dare it violate my brother's sacred place! How dare it resist my strength! With more strength than I ever knew I had, I angrily beat the ground around it until a definite shape started forming. My hands became the shovel as I scooped up enough dirt to lift a steel box to freedom. The thick leather straps didn't budge easily. David's spirit floated right by me and wrapped itself all around me when I forced the lid open that had been tightened with time. I thought I was losing my mind as I stared at the money and the gold bars that sat on top of papers. For the first time I saw before my eyes, freedom papers with the names of David Ricks, Sr. and Clyde Ricks. They had each paid $7.50 for their freedom. There were papers proving they owned the land we lived on. No wonder some folks hated us. On the bottom was a folded paper addressed to me. Scanning them with my eyes wasn't enough. I was compelled to read the words out loud. I sat in a cold, damp, deep, dark, death hole and found peace in the midst of calamity and sorrow."

Daddy unfolded the piece of paper he'd been holding that entire time. He took a deep breath and began to read to Monroe.

Dear John,

Father wanted to be sure Daphne and Adeline have the finest trousseau. They've been surrounded by good men and will chose good husbands. Don't worry about them. Mother's pain from her grief has been draining the life out of her ever since our father disappeared. Nothing of this world will ever make her better. She has very little strength left to fight with. If you're reading this letter, she has another reason to be sad and has already willed herself to die. Make her remaining days comfortable. The reaping of sweat, tears and years of our labor, is yours. Like our father and me, you certainly did your part in sowing. Know that a better day is coming and white men won't think you must bow to them. Read your Bible. 'Cast not your pearls before swine. Forgive those who trespass against you and let vengeance belong to God. What the Bible says is right. Every man must reap whatever he sows. Even me. I reaped death before my natural time because I sowed death on a sawmill foreman. Don't build an impenetrable shell around your soft, pure heart like I did. If you build a shell too tight, nothing can come in and nothing can get out. Strengthen the love in your heart by taking the time to listen to water flowing over rocks in a stream. Rub a flower petal between your fingers and cherish the way it feels. Try not to figure out how a rainbow is made but cherish its colorful hues. Let your eyes worship the grey and cloudy as well as the crystal, blueness of the sky, the majesty of the clean air of spring nights as well as the fierceness of a hurricane, the octaves of a melody, the magnificent, inevitable rising and setting of the sun and moon and the glittering and shimmering of a falling star. Have the kind of hope that whatever you wish will come true. 'Depart from evil and do good. Seek peace and know it.' Follow the commands of your heart, not the fleeting desires of your head. You'll know when every time is right and just what you're supposed to do. Knowing how everything has a season, you must wait for the season of love. Let your spirit taste a genuine love for all things you desire and you'll love forever. Even death can't restrain a loving spirit. Take these lessons with you. Pass them to your children to save your life and theirs' forever. I love you, brother.

DAVID

"We buried David under his precious, Palmetto tree. Mother soon shed her body fat, her hair and what little was left of the artificial glow she reserved just for her children. She was so generous that she spared us the pain of watching her die. One morning, without the least bit of warning, she just didn't wake up."

Monroe's face looked sad.

"Neighbors paid their respects and I buried Mama close to David. I lay awake nights listening to horses' feet and men's angry yelling passing our house in the middle of the night. I could see flickers of fire in the distance. Daphne and Adeline watched me prepare for whatever was yet to come. I oiled the squeaking out of the gates and doors. I cut enough wood to last several seasons. The new mare stopped resisting her fate while the old one accepted hers without a squabble. Malachi's hoofs sparkled with new metal. I waited for the right time and the time was right. David told me I would know. I felt so sad about everything that had already happened and about feeling what was going to come if I weren't obedient. The lessons I'd been taught were becoming clearer. I saw the despair in my sisters' eyes. They were feeling something too. The riders in the night were coming too often. Something about the day of Mother's funeral told me, this was the right day. I could hear it in Daphne's voice when in front of all of those people she told me, 'John we have completely run out of soap. You need to go to town to get some. I looked at her and Adeline and saw haunting messages coming from her eyes. Their grief was wretched. As I was about to depart for town, in front of the people, I told them it was time to make old things clean and new again. I told them I loved them."

Daddy started rubbing on the paper the letter was written.

"Adeline was out the door right behind me, her face looking like a pleading child's. She pulled a package out of her pocket that was tied with the prettiest blue ribbon and handed it to me. Daphne called from the door."

"Don't open it yet!"

"The closer she got the better I saw her tears. Adeline stroked Malachi."

"Wait until you're lonely then open it."

"I was sure that was the last time I was going to see my sisters. Climbing on that wagon that day makes me feel the same pain today. Before I ordered Malachi to step, I reminded them how death cannot restrain a loving spirit. Daphne waved one more time before she slipped backwards into the house. She wouldn't have been able to hide our secret from the guest mourners in the house if she'd watch me leave. Adeline walked down to the palmetto tree and took a seat between our mother's and David's graves. She looked up at the sky and at me pointing to it. I'd never seen such deep blue and there was not a cloud to be found. I could hear her cry as I moved slowly on down the road.

"She yelled", "This weather doesn't match the way I feel. They killed David. My father left one day and didn't come back. John has to leave never, ever to come back. I want terrible things to stop! I want a new day!"

I turned to look back when I heard a rustling sound. The palmetto swayed briskly. Flowers from the two graves made a whirling circle, swirling and twisting until they arranged in a perfect line formation, chasing me down the road. I wasn't ready to disturb the beautifully wrapped package my sisters gave me until I watched the flowers landing right on top of it, commanding me. I ordered Malachi to stop. I untied the bow and unfolded the wrapper. Bless my soul! There was a coal-black braid looking as if life was still flowing from it. Then, I understood why Daphne had her head covered with a scarf for all those days. As if embedded in the hair, there lay undisturbed was Adeline's glossy, gold locket reflecting radiance. I'd never known the piece being from around her neck since my daddy gave it to her. As the other petals circled the wagon, I could feel Adeline's eyes on me. I didn't turn around that time. Instead I raised my arm, pointing again to the sky. I wanted her to capture in her memory how blue it was the day I left. I wanted her to feel, I was aware that I was carrying their most precious possessions with me. I wanted her to know that I knew those, circling, swirling, colorful petals falling in the wagon with me represented things touched by God's mighty hands that we had been taught to love and respect and along the way wherever my journey took me, I was going to be protected by a living, ever-loving spirit. That same spirit was going to protect them too. When the urge hit me to look back again, I turned one last time to see Adeline walking toward her clover patch. I didn't look again but heard her laughing. I knew she'd found her four-leaf clover for the day."

Daddy shared his sacred place and a Ricks secret with his friend. He didn't know he was also sharing the secret with me. I wanted to cry out to Daddy for the relief I was feeling but couldn't. I didn't want to invade the essence of the uniting of spirits. That day, two men bonded forever. Do you see? My windows are like Daddy's tree stump which is like the ground nurturing a palmetto tree that belonged to my uncle David. That day when I heard what the Rick's secret was, I was born again. I twisted my own coal-black braid and held it in my mouth. My own spirit was all twisted in there with theirs'. By the time Daddy finished his story, Monroe was standing over him.

"Nobody's going to hurt you here, John. I won't stand for it. I'll go to my grave with the secret. Besides it wasn't you that killed somebody. It was your father and brother."

"The Bible says we pay for the sins of our fathers. I'm only afraid of what I feel within me. The feelings I had the night before David was killed were the same ones I had the day of that terrible storm and I remember the same anxiety at another time when I didn't heed. I was disobedient. I worry about what that sin will do to my children."

"What does that mean, John?"

"I allowed the fleeting desires of my head get in the way of the commands of my heart."

TEN

I want to go to God as clean as I can. Being obedient keeps my soul purified. Teaching Daddy's lessons to my children keeps me and will keep them on a straight path to heaven if they're obedient too. Unselfish prayer is another way to get there. I used to hear Daddy pray. That's how I learned. I don't pray for myself so much, but I pray for my children all day. I even prayed for them while they crowded my womb before they ever took their first breaths of life's sweet and stale air. I didn't ask God to make them perfect but asked that whatever Thy will, let it be done. I prayed that whatever I was given, I'd take and whatever was taken, I wouldn't question. Something within me must have led me to that prayer because four of my boys were taken before their eyes opened to the daylight. I said if that was what was willed, I even had to be grateful for that. I learned a long time ago that God grants the secret desires of the innocent and even of babies. My little boys knew before they got here, they didn't want to stay. They wanted to be right back there with God.

Grandma Caroline and Daddy said we were perfect children. Neither, Willie, Carl, Aaron or I caused problems from our mother's womb. It wasn't like that the fifth time Mama was pregnant. She was sick all the time. The only time I saw her out of bed was to use the slop jar. Grandma Caroline stayed with us and Vee helped a lot. Grandma said if Mama didn't move around more, that baby was going to stick to her insides. When I heard that, I started to wonder what that baby was going to stick itself to. Hearing that made me begin to wonder how babies got out anyway. I thought if Mama's mouth hadn't been so small and as much as she vomited, maybe she was going to throw that baby up.

Grandma didn't know what she was talking about, after all because that baby didn't stick to Mama. My new little brother Percy woke us up screaming in the middle of the night and never stopped very much for the rest of his life.

I heard Daddy tell Monroe how worried he was at the shrill in Percy's piercing cry. He'd heard that sound before. Said it was like the sound he'd heard coming from me when I was two months old, the year of the 1907 storm.

Mama, Daddy, Vee and Grandma Caroline were just about exhausted from taking turns during the nights trying to console Percy. No amount of nurture or nourishment made him content. We took long naps during the day after being awakened most of the night. It was no wonder we all slept long into the morning one day. Knowing it was well past Percy's middle of the night cry and his feeding, the daylight scared me when I stirred.

I tipped to the crib and touched Percy. My bare feet were chilled from the morning's cool breeze. Warm, glaring sunlight coming through the window didn't raise the temperature on the hand that touched my little brother. The texture on Percy's skin was strange. I shook Mama awake. Her feet hit the floor with urgency. The daylight startled her too. She reached for a towel to soak up the draining sustenance that was to have nourished Percy hours before. She winced at the pain in her gorged breast. At the same time her eyes were questioning.

Percy was much too still. There was an uncharacteristic peacefulness in this usually discontented child. There was also an uncharacteristic peacefulness in our usually, noisy house until Mama screamed. Daddy jumped out of bed, took one look and snatched Percy from his crib, held him and prayed.

"Cry my child! Please cry! You won't annoy us if you cry! In the name of my mother Clyde, please, please, my son, cry!"

Daddy must have been having flashbacks to the morning Grandma Clyde didn't wake up. Mama was turning around and around crying and mumbling. Daddy fell on his knees with Percy in his arms. I fell on mine right beside him.

He prayed, "God put the breath of life back in my child's body. What have we done? What have we not done? It has to be our fault. Forgive us, Percy, my son!"

Carl ran all the way to tell Monroe and Vee about the chaos erupting in our house. If it had been a race, Monroe and Vee would have won. They outran Carl by a mile. Monroe had to almost pry that baby out of Daddy's hands.

For the first time, death had come to our house. Grief lingered. When Mama felt pain from the milk swelling in her breast, she wailed. She blamed herself for sleeping too soundly that night. She started to blame Daddy instead of herself. She said if Daddy had kept a fire burning, Percy wouldn't have been so cold. She said they must not have loved Percy enough. Said her children were perfect and shouldn't die as babies.

Mama fussed at Daddy. Daddy kept talking to God. One didn't talk to the other. Percy was dead. Mama kept crying and we not understanding either of them just kept loving both of them and Percy.

Daddy soon found comfort in his prayers. He cuddled and kissed Mama's pain and tears away. He soothed our troubled minds with what we understood as stories of heaven.

Daddy said, "Percy is happy riding one of those fluffy, white clouds. The smaller you are, the softer and bigger the cloud God will give you to ride all over heaven. The more love we send to Percy, the fluffier his cloud will get."

With that kind of talk, Daddy loved all our pain away.

We lost another boy soon after Percy. His name was Otsey. Grief and pain were no different from the first time. I know now, it had to be that God was giving us a test. When I wasn't on my knees praying, I watched the sky for the whitest, fluffiest clouds in the sky.

In his grief, I heard Daddy tell Mama, "Surely these were God's children. He wanted them back. They were made with God's hands. At least it wasn't men's hands that took them."

When I knelt beside Daddy to pray, I learned not to question God. I learned, what God gives, God can take away. It was God that took my little brothers, not men. When God took my own baby sons, I loved my children's pain away and showed them white, fluffy clouds. I promised whatever God gave to me in my children I'd take without questioning. I want to go to God with a soul as pure and as fluffed up with obedience as the clouds my little brothers and my baby boys ride on.

ELEVEN

Grandma Caroline came to earth just to spoil us. I know it's true because she told me so and whatever Grandma Caroline said was as true as the gospels. It grew in me to know that she was also there to save me. There had to have been a lot done way ahead before the future brought her to me, though. Caroline Walker had to marry Frank Cryer and have Aunt Martha, Aunt Ida, Uncle Stewart, Uncle Oliver and, of course, Mama.

Although Grandma has now been assigned one of the tallest clouds with the biggest fluff, I won't forget how her style was to do everything softly. She walked, spoke, loved, and hugged, all with dignity. She was full of surprises but could never fool me. I knew when the time had been too long for her to come see us. When I knew the time was near, I'd spend most of my days working outside in our gardens. I wanted to be the first to see her sashaying down that long, dusty, Louisiana road leading to our house. She'd be so far away when I'd spot her until she looked the size of an ant. Her sprightly stride and perfect posture made it easy to know it was her. I could see the tall basket balanced on her head without her hands ever touching it. I didn't have to guess. I already knew that basket was brimming with wonderful things to taste, to wear, to play with and some made just to be placed gracefully around our house.

I'd yell, "Here comes Grandma", and little Ricks bodies emerged from the house, off the porch, wherever they resided, sprinting down the road to meet her. Mama brought whomever the baby was to the porch to watch. When Grandma got close enough to protect whoever was our toddler from the rest of us jumping, skipping, happy children, Mama turned the small hand loose.

Grandma waited for us stampeding children to get really close before she lowered the basket, setting it aside to keep us from upsetting her precious gifts. After we all finished getting our hugs, two of us each grabbed a handle to carry the basket the rest of the way home. We all wanted to carry it but fussing over it in the presence of Grandma Caroline never happened. Even though Grandma never raised her voice, we all knew better. We and Grandma talked the rest of the way home.

"You children have the eyes of eagles. How in the world did you see me so far away?"

"Because Sister was watching for you. She's always the first to know", Clyde answered.

"What did you bring us?", Aaron asked.

The excitement of seeing Grandma made us all talk at the same time.

"One at a time, children", Grandma would say. "Don't all of you speak at the same time. That's not polite."

"You're the most beautiful children in the world. And all of you are growing so tall. Each time I see you, Willie, Aaron, Clyde and Sister, you're more like your handsome father."

"You didn't call my name, Grandma. Who am I like?", Carl asked.

"You're about as handsome as any Cryer man ever born and Thelma as pretty as any Cryer woman."

I never got tired of hearing Grandma speak to us that way. She must be speaking the words of angels and was never at a loss for angels' words.

Angels' words make a person freshen up all on the inside. I wanted to hear her talk all the way home but none of us could hardly wait. We either had something to tell her or questions to ask her.

Aaron tugged at her skirt. "What did you bring us Grandma?"

"Something special for each of you."

"Even Mama, Daddy and John David?"

"Yes, John David, your mama and papa."

Clyde, the impatient one's voice sounded pleading.

"Grandma, can you at least give us a hint?"

"Be patient, Clyde. Don't you want to be surprised?"

"No!"

I told Grandma how Clyde wasn't the only impatient one. I was anxious to know too but I was being told more and more by all the adults to be more lady-like. They said being patient was a sign of growing up.

"And such a fine young lady you are, Sister."

I wanted to be a Grandma just like Grandma Caroline. The color of light brown earth, she had a soul as rich as fertile soil. Her hair pulled back in a bun at the back of her head had the appearance of corn silk and the color of pure snow. I wanted soft skin without a wrinkle and a face appearing to display wisdom. When Grandma talked, there were times it was difficult to see her paper-thin lips move. Her smile, as alluring as love itself, if witnessed, drew one inside of her forever. I often went somewhere alone so nobody could see me practicing trying to walk like her and balance a basket on my head. She moved in a smooth glide. It was like a gentle breeze was coaxing her along. I also was attempting to please her all the time, showing off the things she'd taught me.

"Grandma, I finished crocheting John David's sweater. I did it just like you taught me. My sewing is getting much better too."

"I knew you could do it well, Sister."

"I can sew as well as Sister, Grandma", Clyde insisted.

"I know you can, Clyde."

Aaron tugged on Grandma's skirt again.

"Where's Grandpa?"

"He couldn't come this time."

"He promised we'd make bow and arrows. I'm ready to shoot 'em"

"Shoot **them**", Grandma corrected.

"Daddy wanted to show him but Aaron said he'd wait."

"Because I want Grandpa to show me."

"And he will, Aaron. Give him time."

Carl sounding boastful, "Wait 'til you see how much money I made in town selling brooms. People say they like the ones I make better than the ones in the store. Daddy said making them better, I can get a better price. I'M RICH!"

"We helped him", Willie announced.

"Carl, do you share with your brothers and sisters?"

I told Grandma that he did. I knew she'd believe me.

"Daddy said we had to share with each other, and we do."

"There are no finer children in the world."

Grandma believed what she was saying.

We reached the house.

"At last!", Grandma sighed.

Grandma hugged the toddler, whom ever that was and would reach for the baby from Mama, whom ever it was.

"This baby is growing by leaps and bounds", she'd always say, no matter who the baby was.

I wanted the hugs, kisses and other greetings to hurry and be over so the contents of the tightly packed basket could be revealed.

Mama asked, "Where's Daddy. He hasn't been here in a while."

"He's busy and I didn't want to wait around until he could bring me. I didn't mind the walk. It's good for a body to walk."

Mama's mouth was perfect for the task of uttering bad news and bad news it was I heard her say to Grandma.

"You know what Daddy is doing is not right. He's sick and you let him get away with it."

"Your father is not sick. He's just too busy to bring me."

"You let a man gamble away even the very cows your father gave to help feed you. That's sick. First the cows and next it will be the land. Are you going to wait until you're desperately poor before you'll admit it? Then it will be too late."

"It's none of your business, Marjanna. John is taking care of you and these children very well. That's what you should be concerned about."

"I thought, in time, he'd stop but John told me how men like Daddy never stop until they don't have anything left."

"Marjanna, you're speaking about your father."

"And! your husband. "

"How many times do I have to tell you there's nothing you can do about flaws that are born in one. I can give Frank Cryer credit for some good things. He took care of me and his children, including you. He doesn't deserve the kind of disrespect you're showing him. And do you think I'm stupid enough to let myself be deprived? No, I'm not. Your sister and brothers are around. We know how to handle him."

"I'll bet you do."

"That's enough of that kind of talk, Marjanna."

"I need to make you understand."

Grandma refused to say another word about it. She looked annoyed at Mama. Mama's sulking lasted longer than I'd ever seen it.

Grandma came several more times without Grandpa Frank before I saw her and Mama comfortable around each other again. I don't believe Mama would have gotten over the argument when she did if Daddy hadn't told her how disrespectable she looked in front of his children.

If they had let children have an opinion in those days, I would have been on Grandma Caroline's side. She was always on mine and always right. When I came to know that she was to be my savior, she made me remember the conversation she and Mama had about Grandpa Frank that day. Grandma can rest easy on that fluffy cloud, knowing I'm okay. I learned the lesson.

TWELVE

Love poured from Daddy's heart like an overflowing river. His eyes sparkled and twinkled like the stars. His voice was strong as a hurricane's wind and velvety soft. He was quick as a lightening flash and had a smile as bright as summer sunlight. He was tall as an oak and stronger than Malachi.

Most folks didn't see him in the majestic way that I did but most of them liked and respected him. That was enough for him. After he and Monroe Blackburn became friends and Daddy started choosing his friends, he hardly overlooked anyone. Mama made friends too and let us help. I delivered many jars of fruit preserves as well as freshly baked bread to Cora and Eddie Sibley, the elderly couple too tired to work anymore. Daddy took care of Polly Warren's horse regularly taking it to be shod after her brother died and left the horse, his most valuable possession, to his sister. She or her brother never married so she had no one else to help. She made ends meet by leasing that horse for a fee. Daddy kept the animal fed, clean and loved. Wood was stacked high in our shed but Daddy also kept Bernice Bobo's stack replenished after her husband died from being struck by a fallen tree. Doing good for others made Daddy happy. What others thought of him didn't matter. I could feel him feeling good.

Sometime in the evenings, as tired as I knew he was, Daddy still took the time to teach. I never got tired of listening to his lessons that always seemed to teach us something new. There were times when he came home late and I'd be the only one waiting up for him. Even Mama fell asleep before he got home. Maybe that's the reason I learned more of his lessons than everybody else.

The sound of Malachi's hoofs coming down the road was delightful to my ears. It made my drowsy brain come alive. In summer I'd wait for him on the porch. Wintertime found me curled up by the fireplace keeping the fire going so the house could stay warm for him. While I waited, I daydreamed about those Bible stories he told me that made me want to be a Sunday, School teacher. I wanted to tell other children the stories in the same beautiful way Daddy told them to me. His way made me dream of one day to walk where Jesus walked.

There were other times when Daddy and I took long walks and had wonderful talks in the woods. When twigs and leaves crushed under our feet, I'd compose music to the sound and tone of his stories and lessons. He taught me to understand the language of birds and animals which added to the rhythm of my music. The aroma of Daddy's pipe tobacco mixed with the natural smell of earth, pine and wildflowers conjured up mystical illusions in my mind. I'll never forget the first time he told me that death couldn't restrain a loving spirit. He didn't explain the words to me. Neither did he know I'd already heard them while hiding behind a tree listening to him read a letter to Monroe Blackburn from Uncle David. He didn't explain the words but said one day I'd understand them. He said even he was still growing and knowing. He told me I'd have to grow into knowing and had to let knowing grow in me.

Daddy took his pipe from his mouth and stared into its bowl. When he did that I knew a new lesson was on the tip of his tongue.

'Sister, my daddy and my brother David weren't allowed to live their lives fully to the times that were to be their destinies. I often wonder how old they would have gotten. Their lives were cut short because they weren't obedient and because evil is always around us. I'm still alive because I listened to what was speaking to me from the inside. Now, let's speak about you. You were born on the longest day of the year in 1907. That means the time of your life will be long but only if you're obedient. You're my chosen child and I want you, above all else, to remember the lessons I teach you and to be obedient to them. You can be a leader for your brothers and sisters. Remember, a disobedient child won't live half his days.'

Daddy paused to blow blue smoke rings. He stared at the circles. I think he was pondering what lesson should be next.

'One of these days, Sister, I'm go lay down this ole pipe."'

"Daddy, you know you like that pipe too much to quit. I can't remember when you didn't smoke it. I like to smell it. You've smoked so long I'll bet you can't quit anyway.

'Oh, yes I can, when the time is right. All I have to do is watch the moon.'

My mind started getting those illusions again and the music in my brain was going haywire. It always happened when he'd say the strangest things.

'The time of the month when that old moon is waning, all the signs are in our feet. That's the time when we can break old habits. One of these times while that old moon is waning, making way for a new one, I'm going to throw this pipe away and let this good smelling tobacco waste away with it. All of you children were weaned from your mother's breast by the sign of the moon and never did even fret.'

"Are there signs for your head?"

Daddy smiled. I couldn't tell whether he was proud of my asking or whether the question wasn't so smart. Either way it didn't make him hesitate to give me an answer.

'Don't do anything that will make you bleed like pulling a tooth. If the signs are in your head you'll bleed a lot. Wait 'til the signs are in your feet.'

"Look at the moon now, Daddy. There's a halo around it. What does that mean?"

'It means a storm is coming.'

I didn't think he liked speaking of storms.

"There is so much to know. I hope I can remember all these things."

'When the time is right for you to remember, you will. Watch the moon. Don't be fooled by artificial things and artificial men. Believe in what's created by and the words written by God's hands. But also, never underestimate the power of men. The world is filled with goodness, but the devil is busy. Evil is as alive and as powerful in man as is good. Believe in the voice that comes from within you and obey. If you do, evil won't win.'

With that, Daddy's eyes seemed to travel far away. He was silent and his glare ordered me to wait a moment for him to speak.

'Sister, I wish my sisters could see you. You're so much like them. You're smart, beautiful, you're curious and you love everything around you. I wish I could see them. Even now, I want to ask them more questions about some of the things they and David taught me. I want to ask them about waiting for the right time. I want to know if there's more than one right time. I recognize some of the feelings I get in the presence of good, evil, danger and safety and the storms that bring messages to me? They're messages that I can feel.'

Daddy was scaring me. The music in my head became so loud, its intensity roared out of every instrument I'd every heard in my life.

I'd heard talk of two-headed people and fortune tellers. I'd heard Mama and Vee talk about Louisiana voodoo. They talked about a lady named Marie Laveau, who they said was the world's greatest voodoo queen. When we combed our hair, Mama and Vee burned all that was shed so no one could use it to put a hex on us. I don't think Mama and Vee really believed any harm could come to us if we didn't burn our hair. They were just not going to take any chances. But Daddy wasn't speaking about things that had to do with voodoo or two-headed people. His feelings were of something different. He was talking about something deeper and more distinctive. It was something unique to his South Carolina family. Whatever it was, he was trying to pass it on to me. His hands started to tremble the same way I saw them when I hid listening to him read Uncle David's letter to Monroe while he was in the woods, sitting on his tree stump.

'I want to ask Daphne and Adeline if their senses are still growing. Their answer will help me to know about my own. I'm not talking about seeing, hearing, tasting, feeling and touching. They told me about certain feelings, that in due time, I'd understand. They didn't explain what they meant but I think I already know. They can't be explained. One has to feel it. I want to know who else knows. I want to know if it's our family's secret. I want to know whether I'm possessed and if I am, is it with a gift or a curse?'

I had a feeling Daddy wanted to tell me more but couldn't. Then one day a drumbeat rolled in my head. It grew in me to know that day when Daddy was telling Monroe about how he allowed the desires of his head to over-rule what was gnawing on the inside of him, he was speaking about marrying Mama. Now I know, my daddy is the only man I've known to have eaten forbidden fruit and to take responsibility for its consequences. Makes me think my Daddy was even bigger than Adam.

THIRTEEN

Daddy was always the first one up on Sunday mornings. He helped Mama get all of us ready for church. Mama wanted him to be a church big wheel and sit with the deacons. She said he should accept becoming a deacon like the minister had asked but he told Mama that wasn't what he needed. He said there was plenty of time for that. He sat in the Sunday, School room and in the church service with us. Said he wanted to sit with

his family especially while we were still children.

One Sunday of the year was a special day. That day was called Homecoming Sunday. "What a time!" What a Time!" That's what the people said over and over after the Homecoming celebrations at Crystal Springs African Methodist Episcopal. At first, I thought the celebration was just about death and a cemetery. I didn't understand how anybody could celebrate death especially with all the sadness I felt after my little brothers died. I was sorrowful about not just my brothers but for all the people buried in that place. Somebody dying because they were sick or very old and it seemed like it was their time to die was easier to understand than a lady giving birth to a child then dying because of it or a young father being crushed by a tree as he was cutting wood to build fires to keep his family warm or babies like Percy and Otsey that never had a chance to live. But to Louisiana folks, it seemed death was as acceptable as the tumultuous storms and the sulky, summer heat. I'd heard Mama and Vee talk about tuberculosis and dysentery killing a lot of people. Every now and then I heard them say how others were concerned about a person dying from grieving too much over some body else's death. Hearing about something like that was unusual. Death was certain but at times didn't seem to be natural.

Every year the church cemetery got bigger. Before that special June Sunday, the men came to clear more land to make space for new burials that would come the next year. Other family members made sure their folks' graves were presentable. Graves had to be decorated. The cemetery came alive with every color and kind of flower and the people at Crystal Springs Church celebrated their own Decoration Day. The fourth Sunday in June was the day they all came to honor their dead.

Unlike other reverently, quiet Sundays at Crystal Springs A.M. E. Church, worship services on Homecoming Days were filled with boisterous pleasures. There was no mourning. Even the church walls seemed to come alive. We honored the dead, faced the losses, reflected on precious memories, and reinforced our faith. What a time! What a time they had. They deserved a good time. After all, planning for the fourth Sunday in June took 364 days.

The day came on one of those fourth, Sunday June mornings when it began to occur to me, with Daddy's help that there were more important things in the world than what the celebration was about. He watched me watching dark clouds forming. I wanted the rain to stay away so getting to church wouldn't be delayed. Just about everybody was going to be there and I could show just how well I could play the piano and sing. Mama wanted me to. That morning as I watched those frightening clouds, I smelled dust in the wind sweeping across the porch. My gaze was so concentrated across the horizon at the heavy laden, dark clouds that I missed the sight of Malachi standing staunch while Daddy brushed more shine in his black coat. I was more intent on being disappointed at the threatening appearance in the sky and how some people might stay home because of it. I wanted to be heard playing and singing. It was going to be the first time for some to hear. Not showing me off was going to bother Mama the most but I wasn't in the mood to think about her disappointment. I was too busy trying to tolerate my own. Daddy interrupted my concentration.

'What are you praying for, Sister?'

Daddy acted like he could read my mind, the way I thought I could read his. He walked to the porch where I was standing.

'Sit down here with me.'

"Why does the weather have to be looking like this today? If it rains its going to spoil everything", I whined.

Daddy looked at the sky like he hadn't noticed but I knew he'd already witnessed its threat. He lit his pipe allowing light, blue smoke to rise in graceful circles over our heads.

"Be careful what you pray for, girl and always look for the bright side of things. Look over there', he said as he pointed. 'There's what I'm talking about. See the blue sky cradled boldly beside those heavy clouds. There's enough blue sky up there to make a pair of breeches."

His saying that made me laugh. I measured the blue patch with my eyes not wanting to think about breeches right then. I'd never made a pair. I had to remember the size of the patch and ask Grandma Caroline about it later. My eyes returned to the direction of the sky's greater area of dreariness.

"That's all the blue sky needed for God to completely uncover the sunlight. Only God can do that. You can't wish the clouds away. Don't balk at what you can't change. Remember who made the sun and seasons. Don't forget, God also makes the storms. Storms can even come raging in our hearts and sometimes they come with strong winds. Those winds blow in directions that make for change. If you pay attention, you'll know whether your heart is full of sunshine or clouds. The day I was leaving South Carolina, gusting winds from my mother and David's graves blew flower petals down the road landing in my wagon. I had two feelings that day. It was as if I had two hearts. One heart was filled with sunshine and the other with heavy, dark clouds of a brewing storm. Loving spirits were alive guiding me to safety and toward my newest destiny. The other feeling was gloom and dark shadows hovering over my heart telling me that I'd never see the place I was born or Daphne and Adeline again. The day Aaron was born a brewing storm made me uneasy and yet I could discern peace. My clear thoughts were clouded because Monroe Blackburn is white, and I didn't want him forcing his way into my life. It was that stormy day that I discovered the secret in my heart telling me how wrong I was about Monroe. For us, there are secrets in storms and what I can tell you is what David told me. You'll have to learn to understand the feelings you get during a storm's wrath and always search for that patch of blue inside you like the patch that we see now in the sky. The patch needs only to be enough to make a pair of breeches. Be obedient to these rules and you'll find the secrets. And when it's storming, listen to the rhythm of the rain as it composes songs to the rhythm of the beats of our hearts."

FOURTEEN

Mama called out from the front door, "Willie! Carl! Aaron! You all help your father. Sister! Get a move on! You and your Daddy know there's more to do this morning than sit on the porch talking."

"Yes ma'am", I answered.

Daddy beat the leftover tobacco out of his pipe as we both got up. Mama stepped backwards inside the door lowering her head, shaking it disapprovingly while noticing how fast we were going to move to her commands.

None of us needed much coaxing on Homecoming Day. My brothers and I knew the faster we got things done, the sooner we'd be on our way to church. The exciting part for children was knowing we could eat as much of anything we wanted, play as long as we wanted and do just about anything else we wanted after the church service was over. I was eight years old that year. I'll always remember that was the year I learned not to want to do things for the wrong reasons, like wanting to sing and play the piano just to show off. Still I was excited about doing it for the first time.

When Daddy came in the house, he started organizing supplies and the food in the order he wanted my brothers to load the wagon. Mama stood watching, shaking her head when he grabbed another sack of peanuts to throw on the pile.

"John, that's enough food. It isn't necessary to pack anymore. You already have enough food for almost everybody at the church."

Daddy didn't stop getting more.

"These children are going to waste more than they're going to eat."

"I'd rather see it wasted than have my children want for something I didn't bring. You should want the same thing."

"There's a difference in them having what they want and what they need. Sometimes you go overboard with these children."

"What's wrong with that? That's what I'm supposed to do! A day like today is special to them. They're my children. If I don't go overboard for them, who else will? Not even you and they're your children too."

"What are those words suppose to mean? Are you telling me that I don't care as much about the children as you do?"

Mama's voice was getting louder with each word.

"There are times I wonder."

Daddy's answer sounded sarcastic to me. I got worried. This was a day we wanted to stay excited and happy, but my parents were arguing about, of all things, their children. I wasn't surprised at Mama, but it wasn't like Daddy to speak with an angry tone.

Without another word from either of them, Daddy held his fist in the middle of his chest like he felt the weight of a brick on the inside. He stopped filling the sacks, walked out the door and in the woods where I could no longer see him. I knew he'd gone to sit on his stump.

I began to wonder what in the world was wrong with Mama. Other mothers couldn't do enough for their children. Many would have given much to have a man like my daddy. Daddy helped Mama with everything that had to do with us. I didn't understand her acting like there was something wrong with him taking care of us. I wished for the answer. I prayed for peace to come to our house and that our special day wouldn't be ruined.

When Daddy came out of the woods, I could see he was trying to hide his feelings. Big, heavy clouds formed inside my heart and in daddy's heart too. I reached deep inside myself searching for a patch of blue.

FIFTEEN

Daddy and Mama acted like they didn't want to touch each other so I sat between them. The argument they had earlier was still festering with sustained, ill-feelings in both. I didn't care. I liked the grown-up feeling I had sitting up front in a new place on the wagon. Willie, Carl, and Aaron's long legs dangled off the back of the wagon. While seeing their heads bobbing together, I knew they were whispering about their mischievous plans for the day. Every now and then when the wagon hit a bump, Mama turned to look and called their attention to stabilizing our pots and kettles brimming with ice cream custard and all our other food. Clyde and Thelma sat on top of bursting sacks full of peanuts, berries, teacakes and anything else Daddy could stuff in. John David slept in Mama's arms most of the way. I clutched the bundle of flowers I was holding close to me.

I could tell we were getting near the church as the steady, warm country breeze diminished the fiery temper of the sun as it blew the aroma coming from smoking pits of the early arrivals. The smell was tantalizing to the noses of all of us that had now become a caravan of wagons. One of my prayers had been answered. The threatening clouds had disappeared making enough blue sky to make breeches for the whole world.

As Malachi brought us closer, we could see the glistening, white church steeple appearing as if it was rising from the ground and being lifted by the wooden church. I don't know whether it was man or nature that carved the giant, oak, tree-lined path that led to the church. Sights and sounds on the road were something to behold. Young, old, men, women and their children, everybody came. Even well-behaved family dogs, some riding and some trotted beside their wagons. The sound of laughing children mingled with the smell of smoking meat. Bernice Bobo and the widow Parram rode in the wagon with Cora and Eddie Sibley. Polly Applewhite's horse wasn't rented that day. She rode along by herself. Malachi's high steps proudly carried us on. The upbeat tempo grinding on the road made turning wagon wheels sound happy.

Just like us, other Washington Parish families worked diligently getting ready. With new life among them, they came on this special day to pay tribute to lives that had once been. They came to crowd into spaces for the living. That was the day I noticed how our picnic space had grown larger than the space the church reserved for burying the dead. Maybe death wasn't winning.

Once the full site of the church came into my view, I felt peace in spite of the way Daddy and Mama acted toward each other. The peace must have been made as I watched the beauty of the cemetery come alive, right in front of my eyes. An array of color in different kinds of flowers placed by early arrivals covered the graves. The more people arrived, the more the ground swelled with beauty. Daddy didn't have to tell me how all the beautiful colors that created a bouquet were symbols of life. Surely the souls of the dead were being called forth to mingle among us, the living.

Even before Malachi stopped the wagon, I felt a spark at my back pushing me ahead and another one in front drawing me forward. I couldn't have stopped myself if I'd wanted to. I ran straight to my little brothers' graves. I was content that Percy and Otsey weren't buried on top of the ground like Daddy said they buried the dead in New Orleans. Bodies needed to go back to the dust and once again be a part of the earth.

I wished Percy and Otsey had lived long enough for me to help take care of them. I took care of John David a lot. I felt cheated that they didn't live to be old enough for me to know how their voices sounded.

My fingers burned as I dug and planted with my bare hands and spoke to the tiny graves. I told my brothers everything I could think of that happened since the last time I was there. Percy and Otsey weren't really dead. Their spirits were all around us thriving in every beautiful, living thing. I was determined to keep them alive. I patted the ground and spoke to the air around me vowing never again to wait for Homecoming Day to visit. From now on my self-appointed task was to visit them every Sunday to call forth their spirits to keep my brothers' alive.

'I'll be with you.'

Daddy scared me! I was too busy to notice him watching me. He'd read my mind again. He took me by my dirty hands and pulled me up.

"Sister, death CANNOT restrain a loving spirit."

SIXTEEN

Willie, Carl, and I helped Daddy set up the spot he'd come a week earlier to stake out. Mama wanted our reserved place to be as close to the church as we could get so everyone passing by could see her fine things. She was concerned about what we ate with more than what we consumed. She was the only one that brought a linen tablecloth and napkins, the best china, crystal, and silverware to show off at a picnic. If we were at home, she would have stood guard over us to watch the way we handled her finery. At the picnic she was too busy socializing and boasting to supervise.

John David was the spitting image of Daddy. Showing him off was Mama's way of reminding everyone of just how handsome Daddy was. She didn't wait for others to offer compliments but said John David was her and Daddy's greatest creation. I thought my other brothers were just as handsome, but she didn't mention their names. She pointed, calling the rest of us her smart and beautiful children. She encouraged those who may not have intended to come into the church service to come in and listen to me play and sing.

The shrill of the organ's sound coming from the open windows hurts my ears. The sound announced to the busy, gleeful crowd that the church service was about to begin. Worshippers filing through the crowded doors were mostly women and some children having to be coaxed inside by their mothers. Some of older boys with their parents' permission had reached a milestone, being allowed to stay outside with some of the men to finish getting things ready for the picnic. Willie, Carl, and Aaron were among them that year. I wondered why it was just boys who could do certain things. If my friend Starcie Blackburn could have come with us we could have talked about it. I couldn't talk about it with my own sisters. Clyde and Thelma were too young to understand. Starcie and I together could have persuaded our fathers but never our mothers. This wouldn't have been a good day to ask permission anyway. There had already been too much of a disagreement between Mama and Daddy.

John David's bright, brown eyes were wide open. He squirmed in Mama's arms trying to look in the faces of all the people going inside. Clyde and I each held one of Thelma's hands. I turned around to look back at our picnic space. Willie and Carl were trading places to turn the crank on the ice cream freezer. Daddy sat his jar of lemonade down so he could fan pesky flies and straighten the tablecloth. I was trying to determine how soon he'd be ready to come inside but didn't know whether he thought my brothers were completely ready to be left alone. He didn't want our meat to burn and neither did he want to miss my Homecoming Day contribution. I wanted him to be proud.

I didn't see Aaron and wondered where he could have been. I thought maybe he had already gone inside to get a good seat in full view of the minister. Mama boasted that Aaron was their child that was going to be a preacher. He remembered Sunday sermons verbatim. We were probably the only family in Washington Parish that heard him recite the same Sunday sermon twice on Sunday and everyday the rest of the week.

The rows in the back closest to the doors filled up with men who needed to tip in and out to keep their eyes on the church grounds and a check on their food but most of them remained standing. Some tipped in and out to sip home-brewed liquor disguised in fruit jars they hid in their wagons. They drank their own and sampled others'.

Looking out the window, I saw men gesturing from the woods for others to join them. We all knew what they did in the woods and I wondered why they chose such a sacred day to drink and gamble. Those things were much too ugly to be done on holy ground but such behavior should have been expected since Homecoming Day was for any kind of person who was honoring the dead no matter whose dead it was. The way to pay homage was left to each family whether I thought it was disgraceful or not. And besides, there were others that didn't drink, smoke or gamble but they could really curse and they never showed up to church until the fourth Sunday in June.

Sunday service on Homecoming Day was different from any other. Usual services were quiet and done in the same order Sunday after Sunday. But that day, anybody that wanted, for as long as they wanted, in whatever manner they wanted, paid whatever kind of tribute they wanted, to the dead. If ever godliness and patience were to be tested by the presence of the minister, this was the day. There were duets, quartets, sextets, octets, and solos some lasting for as long as fifteen minutes. There were mini piano recitals, a harmonica group accompanied by somebody playing strings in a tub. Things could get so loud, I thought, surely the dead may have been awakened. Mama said, by all means, I should be dignified and if others disturbed the peacefulness of the dead, I was determined to quieten their spirits.

At last it was my time. I saw Daddy standing by the door. His eyes met mine and were encouraging and filled with anticipation. I played softly and sang:

"Precious memories

How they linger. How they ever flood my soul.
In the stillness of the midnight
Sacred, secret scenes unfold.

SEVENTEEN

Daddy met me at the church doors and gave me a big squeeze. I knew I'd done my performance well. We walked to our picnic place while Mama lingered behind with Thelma, Clyde and John David. She wanted to hear and even solicited praises about me.

'Didn't my girl play well? I didn't know myself how excellent the tone is in her voice. That girl practices day and night to have every note just right. She's going to take over the piano in Sunday, School soon. Don't you think so?'

"What a time! What a time!", most would answer.

Daddy and I watched Mama from our table as the people came out. Mama's teeth were so visible that if we didn't know better, we would have thought she didn't have a mouth except we could hear it. She bragged about simple things.

"Willie, Carl and Aaron cook better than John. Come on over to our table if you run out. We have more than enough. You know, Sister and Clyde helped make the custard for the ice cream. They're so good at it, next time they can make it without me."

Clyde and I had only watched her make the custard. We didn't touch it. Our small hands couldn't handle the stirring of that big batch of custard she made.

Mama made sure each stranger knew us and Daddy. She acted like she loved us more when we were around other people. She twisted John David around in her arms so she could put her hand on Clyde and Thelma's heads to identify them. Daddy and I watched her long fingernail pointing toward us and Willie. She peered over the crowd trying to spot Carl and Aaron. She spotted Carl standing at somebody else's picnic table but couldn't see Aaron. Neither could we.

Daddy was embarrassed at times but had long since become accustomed to Mama's ways. That very morning, they argued about how much food Daddy was bringing to the picnic for us. Now she was inviting others to eat some of that food she'd complained about even though everyone had bought enough of their own food. Most of her words and actions had to do with how much more popular she wanted to become. She wanted to have more and better than anyone else. Her children had to be the smartest and as she said, be the best-looking children in Washington Parish. I wonder what she would have done if I'd made a serious mistake on performing or if I'd frozen from fear and not have been able to perform at all. One thing Mama said, I thought, was the truth. John Ricks was the most handsome and smartest man around but even with that, he was proud of us in a different way than Mama.

Daddy's love and care for us was because we were his children. We were a part of him. We were Rickes with rich, Rick's blood flowing just like what was in him. Whatever we did or didn't do, he loved us in spite of it. Sometimes his love and patience was tested the way it was on that Homecoming Day. Just like the minister on every Homecoming Day, he'd be forced to search deep for his own godliness on that particular Sunday.

We watched but couldn't see clearly from where we stood the small objects Carl was tossing. We saw three children sitting quietly watching and not taking part. The gathering crowd made us curious, so we moved closer. Right away Daddy and I recognized one of our peanut sacks and Carl's hand full of teacakes. He was throwing peanuts and pieces of Mama's brown-edged teacakes toward the children who sat huddled together. The girl appeared to be around nine, the same age as Carl. We had passed her walking on the road toward the church looking as happy and as proud as everybody else. Now she cuddled close to two crying, younger boys who we found out were her brothers, all being humiliated.

Those not already near the scene observed the rest of the crowd gathering and Daddy moving forward making them move closer too. Wearing a devilish smirk and so engrossed in his devilment, Carl didn't notice Daddy coming speeding his walk to a trot and me keeping right up with him. Before he noticed us, we got close enough to hear what he was saying.

"You hungry? Have a peanut. Want a teacake crumb? Y'all look hunger. You all look dirt poor. Look at me. I'm rich 'cause my daddy's rich. Your daddy is a drunk."

Daddy grabbed the sack of peanuts and yelled, "CARL! What in the world are you doing!"

"What does it look like I'm doing? I'm offering them something to eat. Don't look like they have much. Don't they look hungry to you?"

I saw Mama walking fast, fast, fast, so fast her skirt danced around her ankles. Curiosity covered her face appearing like she didn't have a clue that the calamity was about her own precious, perfect family. With John David dangling from Clyde's side, she couldn't keep up with Mama.

Mama made it just in time to witness members of her own family in the middle of the chaos and to hear Daddy's next question.

"How could you be so cruel?"

"They're trash. You know it for yourself. Mama already told us folks like these are like the scrapings of the earth. Their mother is a strumpet and their daddy is a drunk. I know it's true 'cause I heard Mama say it."

He saw Mama standing there.

"Aren't they dirt poor Mama?"

Mama put her hand on her forehead looking sick. She didn't speak.

The crowd started to mumble, and the noise rapidly got louder and louder.

Daddy grabbed Carl's shirt and started dragging him through the shocked crowd. The only time I'd ever seen Daddy that angry was a time I heard him speaking to a census taker and of all things, I'd never seen him forcefully touch anybody, much less, one of us.

As tightly as Daddy held on to Carl's shirt, he was no match for Mama. She snatched Carl right out of Daddy's grip turning his face toward her, pulling his collar tightly around his neck with one hand while slapping his head and face with the other. Her big hand went from closed to open. I saw where one of those long fingernails open the skin on Carl's cheek and her fist made his nose bounce to one side.

Daddy yelled, "Marjanna! Marjanna! Get a hold on yourself!"

I grabbed Mama by her skirt, but Daddy and I weren't able to separate her from Carl until she saw the stream of blood trickling down the side of my brother's face. I didn't think all that was happening was real. My mother was drawing that rich, Ricks blood from my brother. My father as strong as he was, struggling to free his child from the person that helped him make this child while his other children and the minister, the entire church congregation and all the guest watched.

Mama's skirt slipped from my hands. I was glad so I could bury my face in them. It occurred to me that my little sisters and brother must be more terrified than I was. That's when I heard them crying so hard. I looked over at Clyde who was trembling and rushed to take John David out of her arms. I was afraid she was almost ready to drop him right on his head.

"Turn around Clyde. Don't look Thelma."

I actually had to get on the opposite side of Clyde and block her view before she realized what I was saying.

The crowd was going wild. Some stood in awe. Some pushed to get closer. Others laughed hysterically. I heard somebody yell that Mama was going to kill him so I turned to see my brother alive one more time. If Mama didn't kill Carl, his shortness of breath would have.

Daddy finally got a grip on Mama's wrist. Trying to keep his grip was like keeping a hold on the devil. She was still trying to reach Carl again. Her hands slipped through Daddy's sweaty grip making her fall backwards. She landed on the ground with her feet straight up in the air. Her skirt and all those pretty petticoats she was wearing, covered her face. She was gasping for air by the time she fought her way from under the heavy mass of fabric.

A man in the crowd yelled, "John Ricks sho do buy his wife pretty drawers", as the crowd roared with laughter.

While Daddy was helping Mama off the ground, a glimpse from the corner of his

eye caught something familiar coming out of the mass of trees with the gamblers. Aaron's bright, red checkered shirt couldn't have been missed in the biggest of crowd.

When Daddy steadied Mama on her feet he walked toward Aaron. Breath was in short supply that day for my folks. The closer Daddy got to Aaron the more labored his breathing became. His fist tightened. Once Daddy was close enough to touch him, Aaron's sweaty hands opened releasing a pair of dice that fell and rolled stopping at Daddy's feet. A man's voice yelled, 'CRAP!' Drunk and sober men were so tickled they roared and some even choked on their laughter. I thought, so much for having a Ricks brother as a preacher.

I couldn't watch anymore. I'd seen enough hurt for the day. Daddy had too. After all, feeling hurt was the way our day started.

Daddy cautiously looked around to see where Mama was before he reached to take Aaron by his arm. One of his children was already injured by her hands. He wasn't going to let her hurt another one. He saw Polly Applewhite and Bernice Bobo walking toward our wagon on each side holding her up.

Daddy looked at the dice lying at his feet. Slowly raising his eyes, another unfamiliar sight came into his view. He saw dampness in the crotch of Aaron's pants and a urine trickle running down his legs halting and pooling in the top of his socks. As Daddy's long arm reached out for Aaron, he took off running so fast it looked like sparks were coming from his heels. He didn't stop running until he reached the cemetery where he knocked over wreaths, crushed the freshness out of the flowers, scattered ribbons and bows, while kicking down crosses as he disrupted the only remaining peaceful place that had been left quiet on that Homecoming Day.

I thought about how the dead were being disturbed by that loud noise coming from inside the church and how I tried to put them at rest. But now they were disturbed again not by rabble- rousing, non-sanctimonious hypocrites but by of all people, my own brother.

I fed Thelma and Maurice, the only ones hungry, then helped Miss Polly and Mrs. Applewhite pack Mama's beautiful things. We left before the picnic really got started. All the people on the church grounds stood to watch us leave. Rozella Robinson stepped prominently to the edge of the road and watched with a smirk. A harmonica played softly as we started down the road. The sun was behind us letting us view shadows of ourselves.

Mama's sobs were incessant. Willie, Carl, and Clyde snickered. Aaron's embarrassment kept him quiet. Thelma played with John David making him laugh out loud until they both lay down to sleep. I sat between Mama and Daddy keeping a hand on both of them all the way home. We all needed to touch. Turning wagon wheels grinding on the road sounded sad.

What a time! What a time!

EIGHTEEN

Doctor, Doctor, can you tell
Will Little Mary soon be well?
We all need to have her play
And be with us everyday.

Hand-me-downs aren't always in the form of clothes and shoes. Sometimes they come in other forms. Hand-me-downs are usually from top to bottom or from largest to the next down and from oldest to youngest. The Little Mary poem was handed down and was one of the first and the easiest each of us learned but it didn't start at the top. The poem passed from Carl to me, to Aaron, to Clyde, to Thelma, to John David. No one taught us the poem. Like other things, we learned them just by listening.

Willie, the oldest, wasn't skipped on purpose. He struggled with what came easy for the rest of us. He could think it but couldn't say four lines without stuttering except if he said the words so fast, they weren't understood. He tried really hard but wasn't able to avoid Mama's impatience. If she was around his hands trembled when he tried to write. If he made a mistake, she badgered him further into slowing his progress. Willie to her was less than what she thought was perfect. She yelled at his shortcomings.

He embarrassed her because she wanted people to think she and Daddy were incapable of imperfection.

Daddy said Willie hadn't been right since that chimney fell on his head during that 1907 storm. Of course, Daddy blamed himself for it spending many regretful days and was determined to fix my brother. He spent more time with Willie than with the other boys. Willie needed him the most and with the patience of Job, Daddy helped Willie believe he was as smart as the rest of us.

Willie hated school so Daddy didn't make him go there. He allowed Willie to go along with him to teach him things not written in books. If daddy had to teach him to count the same coins a hundred times he didn't quit until his son got it right. Willie went with him to work and learned to do all that Daddy and the other men did. At home they carved animals, repaired gates and fences and made furniture. Willie was beside himself when he finished making a chair the same as Daddy's big chair. Daddy said only a real man could make a man-sized chair. Daddy let Willie place the chair right next to his. It was there the two of them sat side by side. Daddy recited verses from the Bible repeatedly until they were embedded in Willie's mind. It wasn't long before Willie could recognize the words on paper. He started writing the words without his hands trembling even when Mama was present. If she yelled, he ignored her.

Daddy promised Willie his own place in the garden as soon as he learned to spell and write potato, tomato, squash, pepper and whatever else he wanted to plant. Willie earned his plot. The rest of us wanted our own place in the garden too. Daddy said Willie got his own because he was the oldest. Even though he was the oldest, I knew Willie's little plot was not and wasn't going to be a hand-me-down.

Slowly but confidently Willie became independent. The first time Daddy let him go to town by himself was when he felt grown-up and proud. Besides he was the only one except Daddy that Malachi didn't hesitate to obey. Being confident in what he'd been taught made him worship the very tracks Daddy made in the earth. He knew where his earthly help had come from. Eventually he returned to school and kept right up with the rest of us while loving being there.

NINETEEN

Daddy came to school to check on us more often especially after Willie returned and until he was satisfied Willie was settling back in. Some things happen for good and some for evil but everything under the sun has a time and purpose. If Willie hadn't returned to school Daddy might never have come often enough to find out what went on with his children and I would never have told him about our teacher, Miss Rozella Robinson.

Miss Rozella wasn't quite five feet tall. Her noticeable hands were as big as any man's and her tiny feet looked too small to support her short, stocky frame. She was one of many-colored people I knew with hair as red as Vee Blackburn's. The only good thing that came from knowing Miss Rozella was to eventually get to know her sister, Roxie.

The sisters were born in Franklinton, but Mrs. Roxie ran away from Louisiana when she was only 15 years old settling in Memphis, Tennessee. Like some of the other children in Washington Parish, the sisters were ridiculed. They had been told their father was dead and believed it until they became old enough to understand the teasers who said their father was a red-headed drifter who came and stayed in town long enough to spread red-headed babies all over the parish. The night the drifter sneaked out of town, the sisters' mother sneaked away with him. Learning the truth, the absence of their mother and suffering from scorn scarred them deeply. Red hair on a child whether associated with the drifter or not didn't matter. In Franklinton, having red hair was like having a scarlet letter. So, Roxie left.

Rozella, on the other hand, wasn't as adventurous as Roxie. She wasn't brave enough to leave her familiar place and needed to prove to everybody that she had as much worth as anyone else. She set her goals years before she achieved them, studying long and hard to be educated. She wanted to eventually become Franklinton's only teacher. The town needed only one and she'd occupy that spotlight all by herself sharing the glory with no one else. The next thing for her after becoming the town teacher was finding a respectable man to marry making her even more respectable. Meeting both these goals would prove she wasn't a loose woman like the town thought of her mother.

Roxie told me, when Daddy came to town, Rozella wrote her letters claiming John Ricks as her own before she ever spoke to him. Roxie said Rozella wrote, 'If he's as smart as everybody claims he is, he won't be intimidated by my intelligence like these other dumb, Washington Parish men. I'll let him know right away that I'm a teacher. I'm sure if he's all that smart, he'll want an educated woman. Just think, my sister, as handsome as he is, I can give him beautiful, light-skinned babies. I'm smart. He is too. Just think how educated our children will be. Together he and I can teach them everything they need to know. I'll be going in town Saturday to see him. Just you wait. He's going to ask to marry me.'

Roxie told me that Rozella didn't say how she'd hang around in town on Saturdays, going early and staying late hopefully, to see Daddy. Some Saturdays he didn't show up in town at all leaving her feeling stranded. But when he did come she did everything she could to make him notice her. She made up problems so she'd have an excuse to speak to him.

Daddy was polite. He carried her packages and gave as little advice as he could. Daddy acted like he didn't like her.

One day after visiting the school, I heard Daddy telling Mama he couldn't stand to hear that teacher talk. Mama didn't know what he meant. She didn't want him to speak ill about Franklinton's teacher that way. She looked up to people with titles like the preacher, the schoolteacher, the music teacher and the deacons. She wouldn't have believed Rozella had an accent tailor-made for Daddy's ears only. Rozella's words were spoken so fast and sounded so phony that Daddy said half the time he was compelled to tune his whole body in to understand what she was saying. He told Mama how sometimes when Rozella finished talking he needed a translator. When she said John, it sounded like she was saying Jone. She called dollars, doelars. Cents sounded as sunts and mud, mod. In daddy's ears a typical sentence sounded like, 'Jone, I paid three doelars and fufty sunts for thut druss and those chuldrun run by me and splushed mod all over me.' Said he figured out the translation as, "John, I paid three dollars and fifty cents for this dress and those children ran by me and splashed mud all over me." Daddy said when she was speaking, he nodded, grunted, and said "uh huh" in the wrong places. He said he strained his ears so much he was afraid they'd be damaged. He spent as little time as possible in Rozella's presence.

Daddy's reason for his hanging around in town was so he could see Mama. Then the day came when the pin came out of Grandpa's wagon wheel. After that day, Rozella didn't manage to get even the little bit of attention she'd been getting from Daddy. She was humiliated and bitter which grew worse over time. She blamed both Mama and Daddy for being responsible for her not marrying the only man she'd ever had a desire to marry. Now in her letters to Roxie she said Daddy let her make a fool of herself in front of the whole town. She told Roxie how that kind of man in Washington Parish came few and far between.

Rozella felt so betrayed she even spoke to her sister about moving to Memphis, but Roxie had only discouraging words. Told her sister there weren't any jobs for teachers and working at common labor would be beneath her. 'Don't come here', Roxie told her.

Looks like Roxie was stuck in Franklinton without a man. Her bitterness raised evil thoughts. She wrote that there may have been another chance at getting Daddy. Said she had hoped the marriage failed. She wished Mama to be barren. Mama wasn't barren, not by a long shot. Willie was born in less than a year after the marriage and the babies kept coming.

Roxie told me how she could tell the sore in Rozella's heart began to fester as early as when I was born. Daddy boasted about his babies in town. As proud as he sounded about his children and as much as he talked about us Rozella couldn't help but hear. As I got older, I saw how she'd roll her eyes and rush off in the opposite direction when she'd see us.

It was my very first day at school when I felt danger coming from the glare in Rozella's eyes. Something bad was in her voice when she told me how I looked just like my daddy. After my first school day Rozella avoided my eyes, directly. She told me I wasn't as perfect as my "mammy" and daddy tried to make me. Told me she didn't like to look at my face. She searched for faults in me and I tried to actually show some thinking that might please her. I pretended I couldn't spell words I'd learned to spell long before I started to school. Nothing I did, good or bad, kept her from being furious at me. I was scared to death of her, but I didn't want to tell Daddy. What happened at the picnic on Homecoming Day kept him so sad so long I didn't want to ever see him like that again. I tried to tell Mama once. She said I must have done something to deserve what I got, and I wasn't to do it again. When Willie heard Mama tell me that, he started stuttering again. One day Daddy noticed his hands trembling when he tried to write.

"Son is something wrong?"

"I'm just tired of school. I don't want to go back. I'm not learning anything anyway."

"Oh yes you are and I'm proud of you."

"Why does Miss Rozella hate us? She doesn't like any of us but treats Sister the worst."

"I don't think Miss Rozella hates you all. What makes you think it so?"

"One day Sister wet her pants when she was beating her. She said Sister wasn't perfect as you and Mama think. Sister never does anything wrong except wet her pants sometime when she's scared. She told Mama about it but Mama said she must have done something wrong."

"Wet her pants? When did Sister tell your mother?"

"Long time ago."

Our Franklinton parents acted pleased with the learning their children got inside Crystal Springs School and didn't fail to show it. Daddy and the other fathers kept low hanging limbs cut that might fall during those blowing storms. They fixed leaky places on the roof and made extra desks when there weren't enough for the number of children. Our mothers gathered just before school started and even sometimes even after school started to sweep out debris and wipe dust that blew through windows that were seldom closed. Parents kept our one room school comfortable and safe. They trusted Miss Rozella to do the rest. What my brother Willie told Daddy made him anxious.

When Daddy would bear down really hard on his razor strap while sharpening his razor or when he chewed on his unlit pipe to keep from bit-ing his lip, I knew something was making him sad. One morning he even rushed us off to school too early although we had plenty of time.

Before we were good and settled in our seats, I heard familiar sounds. I knew the clickety, clack sound in Malachi's feet. I could distinguish his bray from every other horse's in the whole world. From where I sat, I could see Daddy coming. From where she stood, Miss Rozella couldn't see. I saw my daddy tipping up to the back door and lean against the school building. He didn't come right on inside like he usually did. Daddy had taught me to listen to every sound that was around us and this time I could tell, he was quietly doing the listening. While he stood there, he took his handkerchief out of his pocket and wiped the dust off his shoes revealing a glossy, mirrored shine. He ran his hand through his curly, black hair with his ears still trained on the voice inside. The color of his hair matched the color of his pants and tie. I could see the tip of his brown pipe lying snugly against his snowy, white shirt pocket. Who in the world could blame Miss Rozella for wanting a man looking like him?

When Daddy moved slightly out of my sight, I strained my neck to keep my eyes on him. I wanted to tell Miss Rozella he was there, but she had made me too afraid to speak up. The next thing I remember was Miss Rozella standing at my desk asking why I wasn't paying attention. She walked back to her desk and pulled out her strap that was like the one Daddy used to sharpen his razor.

'Claudie Ricks! Come up here! Turn your back to the class!'

She grabbed my dress by the tail and hoisted it high enough for the other children to see my underwear. That's when my daddy stepped inside. He saw it all. Thank goodness!

Without a hint of emotion, Daddy greeted us, "Good morning children."

Their answer of good morning from the children was in unison. Willie and I both trembled.

"Rozella, let me speak to you outside."

Rozella started to ease the strap toward the floor as if to try to conceal it. Daddy's eyes went up and down from the strap to her face. As it hit the floor he reached down and picked it and started toward the door. He paused allowing Rozella to step outside first. Even in that moment of anger, Daddy was still being a gentleman.

"Rozella if I didn't have sisters, a wife, daughters and hadn't loved my mother, I'd beat you with this strap. It's the respect that I have for other women that protects you from me leaving scars on you on behalf of my Claudie. Don't you ever put a forceful hand on one of my children or any other child and I find out about it. Do you understand?"

Daddy tried not to let us hear but I heard every word. Rozella's bitterness remained in her tone.

"I spank all the children, John. I don't have the time to fool with spoiled brats. Your children are too spoiled, and they aren't any better than anybody else's."

"Yes, they are. They're not animals. I don't hit animals much less my children. You used a razor strap on a human being. Razor straps don't spank. They beat."

Daddy paused as if he was thinking about something. His head laid to one side, straightened as he starred at Rozella.

"I knew you were a phony. What happened to your accent? Listen to this you phony lady. My children aren't spoiled but are certainly loved a lot. You wouldn't know the difference in being loved or being spoiled. You've never had either. My little children as young as they are have already had enough love to last them the rest of their lives. Too bad I can't say the same for you. You're a phony, old spinster who won't ever be happy. But, if you ever put one of your fat, unhappy hands on one of my children I'll be sure no one will ever call you teacher again. I'll let every parent know that you beat the children."

Daddy lifted the razor strap up.

"I'm going to take this strap with me to show what you beat them with. I'll see to it that you never work again in the entire state of Louisiana. Your job is to teach the children. My wife and I will discipline ours."

Daddy's voice had started to tremble and got louder before he finished speaking. It was then he stepped back inside the room. Everyone watched as he beckoned for me to come. Daddy brushed my hair off my brow with one hand and hugged me with the other.

"All is well, Sister. All is well."

I know I was supposed to feel safe at that moment, but I didn't.

Daddy went outside but stayed leaning against it until school was out. I knew he was still there. I could smell the sweet aroma of pipe tobacco floating through the open window. I knew he was still listening.

Rozella didn't teach much the rest of the day. She made us sit still and quietly read. She kept looking at her hands. Most of us stared at and turned the pages but weren't reading or concentrating on what was on the pages. At the end of the day Daddy walked us and Malachi home.

Mama didn't as much as open her mouth to speak when Daddy told her what happened. She pressed her lips together so tight her mouth disappeared.

The next morning Daddy went to work, and Mama came to school. She didn't ask Miss Rozella to step outside like Daddy did. She stood in the middle of the room where everybody could hear.

"Rozella, John told me he came to see you yesterday. He told you not to whip the children. Well, I'm over-ruling John. You're a fine teacher and an upstanding lady in this town. John may not be satisfied but I am.

If you think my children need a beating, including Sister you can give it to them. You don't need John's permission. You have mine."

Mama didn't want to lose favor with the only teacher in town. Teacher like preacher was a name-branded title. Like those others with titles, she wanted her high status to show and not be threatened by her husband's actions. She didn't know Rozella loathed the very sight of her and was in love with her husband. Rozella always avoided Mama as much as she could. Mama thought Rosella was just acting sophisticated. Rozella's smirk that day was obvious.

I could feel a river swelling in my eyes and billows tossing in my chest. That brick in my chest rose as I looked in my mother's angry eyes. I tried to diminish the weight by searching inside myself for a patch of blue. I could find, not even just enough to make a pair of breeches. I couldn't find any. That raging tempest made me weep the rest of the day.

I couldn't tell Daddy what Mama did. Mama didn't tell him either. Telling was going to make him sad again. I didn't want him to ever feel that kind of pain again. I'd bear the pain for him. I promised my brothers and sister I'd do anything they wanted if they didn't tell Daddy what Mama had done. I made them believe Miss Rozella would just beat me again and Daddy was going to be even sadder. I made them put their hands on the Bible and swear.

I could feel that Daddy could feel something was not right. I felt his mind was growing full of doubt about something. On the inside of me I could feel a secret brewing that connected the 1907 storm to that day Mama came to school.

TWENTY

When Daddy started on his journey from South Carolina, he had no idea where he was going. In those times most folks didn't venture too far from the place of their birth. He'd heard of many wonderful places but never thought he'd see them. He said his journey from South Carolina to Louisiana made him see more wonders of God's universe than most South Carolina people ever even heard about. Grandpa David Sr., Uncle David Jr., Grandma Clyde, Aunts Daphne, or Adeline had never even seen the big ocean. Daddy saw it and said the Atlantic was the clearest, biggest, bluest thing he'd ever laid his eyes on except the sky. He said the Mississippi looked wider and muddier than the biggest piece of earth in Louisiana. Daddy survived hail, sleet, snow, scorching heat and torrential rainstorms. He survived the heartbreak of his dead father, mother and brother and having to leave his sisters alone at the time he should have been there to comfort them. Even that didn't take him all the way down. He overcame the fear of having to confront suspicious and sundry strangers. He held steadfastly to the lessons taught by Grandpa David Sr. and Uncle David Jr. He held tightly to his faith and said he saw the power of prayer revealed when there was no sun or moonlight to guide him and when he thought he'd lost his way. Not knowing his destination and the fear of stopping too long to sleep, he trekked on and on until his tired, young body told him he had to rest in Franklinton.

Daddy's entire being was created naturally into pride and bravery. Lessons of love taught by his mother and sisters shaped and molded him. They were given without conditions and taught him to give them back the same way. Rules of life and splendors of the heavens and the earth were passed to him by his father and brother. He was taught how to choose the highest quality of a tiny seed and to plant, nurture, protect and sow it. But now for the first time in my life I think my father had more doubts in his decisions and more questions than answers. Was the decision to stop and stay in Franklinton the right one? Was this the first time he let his head along with his tired body over-rule his heart? Were these the right questions he was asking himself? Did he ever ask himself whether he should have taken the chance and stayed in South Carolina? No satisfactory answers came but if yes was the answer to that last question, we Ricks children wouldn't have been his most precious gifts. But we had him on the inside of us no matter who our mother would have been. I know I did. Weren't we the most precious of all his seedlings he planted and nurtured?

My big, strong daddy had a heart as vast, as strong, and as beautiful as that mighty, blue ocean he told me about. But hearts just like vast, wide, clear, and mighty oceans have their limits. Their waves rise, pulsate, then they ebb, never to rise and be the same wave or to make it be the same water again. Just like the waves of the ocean there are limits to the amount of weight one heart can carry. My big daddy, the first man that I loved, my first teacher, the strongest man I knew who rode the tallest waves of life and weathered just as many raging tempests now carried a heart as heavy and as muddy as that mighty Mississippi River. Now he was carrying a mind that was just as murky. I saw Daddy drowning in doubt. I felt a heavy, evil mist clouding our destinies. Daddy spoke about how he thrived and how he'd survived dreadful things. Now he sensed the most damaging threat to his most precious seedlings: his children. He didn't know how or what was going to happen.

I read danger in my daddy's eyes when Mama eventually told him she went to school and told Rozella to beat us. I tried so hard to be strong, but weakness tore into my heart strings too. I knew he wasn't ever again going to be able to look through muddy water and spy dry land.

Daddy started coming home later and later. I missed him being with us in the evenings, so I started waiting for him on the porch no matter how late it was. I passed the time swatting at bugs daring not to kill or hurt one. Hurt was already taking up too much space around our house. I allowed mosquitoes to feast on my flesh. Their stings kept me awake. I caught lightening bugs and put them in a jar only to set them free once they were too weary to climb to the top. I wished freedom for the lightening bugs the same wishes I had for Daddy and me. God's hands could reach low and lift high. This time his hand had to stretch way down to reach Daddy and me.

It's no telling how many nights I would have waited for Daddy on that porch with the hope of being the first to know of his regaining the feeling of being whole again.

One night I'd gotten so tired I was about to lie on the porch. The sound of Malachi's hoofs broke the monotony of other night sounds. The strange noise of horse hoofs blended with a voice like the croaking of a lone cricket crying in the night. The cricket sounding voice was singing loudly off key. Between the bars of an unblended melody he paused to yell, "Whoopee!" Other words were slurred and incomprehensible. So was the strange behavior. Coming widely awake, I sat up to listen, trying to recognize the approaching stranger who looked like my daddy. I was surprised to find out it was my daddy.

"Hey, my little Sister! Naw! Naw!, Naw!. You're not little Sister. You're my big girl Sister!"

Malachi stopped at the steps without as much as a "whoa". One of Daddy's feet touched the ground. The other foot got caught in a stirrup. He stumbled and fell backwards trying to break free. I leaped off the porch to catch him before he toppled all the way over.

"Daddy what in the world is the matter with you?"

His pipe tobacco smell couldn't hide the rank smell of whiskey or the trouble that was brewing.

"Nothing is the matter. Just got drunk, that's all. YIPPIE! YIPPIE! YIPPIE!"

After that last YIPPIE, Mama, Willie and Carl came out the door.

"John, have you lost your mind!"

"Oh my God!", Willie screamed.

Carl, the only one not appearing upset laughingly said, "Daddy you been sneaking spirits haven't you?" as he jumped off the porch grabbing Daddy just before he tumbled all the way over. I was glad. He was becoming too heavy for me to hold.

"How about that/? Good ole Pops got drunk"

Carl didn't sound half as disappointed as the rest of us looked.

Willie helped get Daddy in the house. Even Malachi was acting hostile. It took a lot of my strength for me to pull him to the barn.

As I closed the barn door, I looked up to see what kind of moon was shining on us. It was new and bright. I could see its dark side and thought that must be the side that holds other signs Daddy hadn't told me about. I wondered where the signs were now that allowed this to happen. Were they in the head, the feet or where? One place I don't believe they were was in the heart. My daddy never acted like this before.

All of us slept late into the next morning. Mid-day light and Mama's loud voice woke me up. Daddy was still in bed.

"You should be ashamed of yourself coming in here over these children and me, drunk! What's gotten into you? Get up from there and answer me, John!"

I didn't like Mama yelling at my daddy. I heard him groan and jumped out of bed running to the door to look. He groaned again and turned over ignoring Mama.

"John did you hear me? I said get up!"

Mama's fussing at him went on and on. I wanted him to have something warm in his stomach. I rushed to make strong, hot tea to have ready when he did get up. I wet a towel to have something cold to wash his face. I wondered if he thought he had made a mistake. Even if getting drunk was a mistake it was nothing like the one Mama made. She told Rozella Robinson to beat me. What kind of mother is that? I know Daddy wasn't thinking his getting drunk would hurt us. The only pain he was considering had been inflicted on himself.

I stood over him holding the cold towel. His eyes barely open, he tried to raise one arm. When he realized it was me standing over him, he managed a faint smile after a startled look. When he tried to sit up his head fell back on the pillow. Whiskey had made my daddy helpless. When he heard Mama's voice again, he closed his eyes and frowned. He rubbed his hand up and down his chest and stomach.

"Why don't you sit up, John? Where were you when you got drunk? What are our neighbors going to think when they here about this? Where did you learn such disrespect? How do you think this makes me feel?

"Mama, do you have to keep yelling at him like that? Can't you see he doesn't feel well?"

"Don't you give me any sass. Do you understand me, Sister"?

I placed the cold towel on Daddy's head and left the room without answering.

Mama followed me in the kitchen. I knew she would. I reached for a cup and saucer to pour tea but before I turned around, I felt a tug on my braid and my whole body being jerked backwards.

"Don't you be disrespectable to me! I'll lay you on this floor", Mama yelled as she whirled me around.

The cup and saucer slipped from my hand hitting the floor. Breaking glass striking the floor and my gasp muffled the familiar sound of a cracking floorboard by Daddy's bed. The look in my eyes must have been what tipped Mama off. Just as she raised her hand Daddy grabbed it tightly from behind and held it in the air before she turned around.

"You better not ever hit her and I find out about it!"

"You let my arm go!"

Daddy's grip on Mama's wrist was so tight I could see the palm of her hand turning white.

"I won't turn loose until you hear every word of what I've waited a long time to tell you. I know you went to school behind my back and told Rozella she could beat my children. If I find out either of you have laid a hand on my children, I'll get Rozella's job taken and I'll leave you and take my children with me. There's no telling what else I might do. You don't have enough sense to know Rozella can't stand you. Rozella wanted me for herself. Everybody in Franklinton knew that but you. You're so busy licking up under her and those other so-called name-branded people you can't see straight. Then you went and gave someone who hates you permission to whip my child. Rozella told everybody that listened what you did and how sorry she feels for you and my children. There's no reason to feel sorry for my children but I don't blame her for feeling sorry for you. I love you as my wife but not so much that I'd let you hurt my children. I love them more than any other thing in this world and don't want to feel that I have to protect them from the rest of the world and their own mother too."

Daddy slowly eased Mama's arm down to her side and was gradually unleashing his hand from her wrist. She snatched herself free the rest of the way and rushed out of Daddy's reach.

"You weren't loving us so much last night with your drunkard self."

Daddy walked away and got dressed. When he left the house, I knew he was heading to his tree stump.

I felt guilty. If it hadn't been for me, they probably wouldn't have had that argument. Well, maybe they wouldn't have had it that day. I grew to know it was going to happen sooner or later. I just wish I hadn't been the one to start it. I would rather have taken that lick across my face. I even felt bad about being disrespectful to Mama. I was only trying to defend my daddy who I thought was defenseless until he appeared in the kitchen.

The tension in our house was so thick Daddy's saw couldn't have cut through it. Monroe and Vee could tell something was wrong. Mama didn't talk about it with Vee, but Daddy told Monroe. I told my friend Starcie. Daddy promised he'd never get drunk again. He kept his promise about not getting drunk but didn't stop taking what he called "a little nip" every now and then.

Daddy didn't like the way we walked around looking sad because of them. Willie started to stutter, and his hands trembled again when he tried to write. Daddy told Monroe it didn't seem normal for a woman to sulk as long as Mama. He tried to make up with her. He bought more beautiful fabric. He picked more berries. He even cooked for us sometime while she lay in bed. He'd never seen his mother or sisters carry on this way. His father or brother hadn't prepared him for this. He kept trying. Mama didn't budge. His little nip helped his smile but didn't diminish the pain in his eyes.

Mama so wrapped up in her sadness following the embarrassment about what Daddy told her about Rozella didn't pay attention when I started wearing the shiny, gold locket on my neck all the time. She never watched when I'd unwrap the package and remove the long, black braid using her mirror to look and compare it to my own. Not listening to anything my daddy said, she didn't hear when he reminded me not to forget the locket and hair represented unconditional love and eternal, living, loving spirits. He went so far as to tell me how I should pass them to my child. He said I'd recognize the one that understood the difference in storms of goodness and of wrath. He said tell your children that death cannot restrain a loving spirit.

It started to be that every time I looked in the mirror at that locket or caressed the softness of the hair in that braid, I saw darkness. The taste of sorrow stayed in my mouth and again I felt thunder rolling in my chest. I heard the wailing cry of crickets and smelled sawdust. A storm of wrath was brewing over the horizon.

TWENTY-ONE

I asked Mama why Daddy's eyelids were puffy and wondered why he had to cut slits in his boots and shoes to make room for his swollen feet. She said it was because he needed to stop drinking whiskey. The more I saw Daddy like that the closer I felt to that locket and braid. On cloudy days I felt as gloomy as the grey sky and Daddy wasn't there all the time anymore to help me find enough blue sky to make a pair of breeches.

To be more afraid of your children being hurt by their own mother than by a tumultuous storm made a little nip more desirous and tastier everyday to Daddy. He used to see us off to school on many days and was home in the evening long before we went to bed. But it wasn't like that anymore. We all still went to church together, but he seldom came inside anymore. I didn't want to think he was hiding whiskey in the wagon like some men did on Homecoming Day. I thought how being weary, wary, and lonely was a disastrous combination. With all those things together, how can a broken heart heal? Daddy's nip eased his pain.

My daddy was suffering and began trying to fool us. The lessons in building, planting, harvesting, finding blue patches in grey skies, whittling and whistling were done with an elevated speed as if he needed to hurry. After a while the whistling became an unsolicited wheeze changing to raspy rattling in his chest. He couldn't raise his arm to point to the blue patches in the sky.

The day was appropriately cloudy when Willie and Carl came running as fast as they could under the weight of carrying Daddy from out of the trees where they'd go to learn or to have fun. Aaron was running ahead of them screaming for Mama. I could see Daddy's mouth wide open, his chest heaving up and down and his eyelids bulging, white and sunken. Each breath seemed like it was going to be his last. I waved to Aaron pointing him toward the Blackburn house to tell Monroe to get the doctor.

Immediately Mama was uncontrollable, standing in the way trembling, screaming saying over and over, "Help me Lord! Help me please!" A prayer for Daddy might have helped us all.

Willie ripped daddy's shirt off while Carl took off his boots. I got fresh water to heat just in case the doctor needed it for herbs.

Word spread about how Willie caught Daddy after he fell to his knees. He and his boys were in a whittling contest. Whoever was the first to finish carving an animal was going to be the winner. Daddy could win if he wanted but always let one of them. My brothers weren't watching Daddy. They kept on shaping and shaving wood until Willie became disturbed by Malachi stomping his hoof and Daddy not paying Malachi any attention. This allowed Willie to look up to see him before he toppled all the way over.

Daddy lay gravely ill but despite that, our house ran as smoothly as if he were running it himself. Grandma Caroline moved in with us and Monroe took charge over everybody. Neighbors and friends came in a steady stream. The widow Parram rode her horse everyday to help Vee with us. Polly Applewhite taught me shortcuts to tending my garden. I still do some of those things right today. Bernice Bobo exchanged clean for dirty laundry. Cora and Ed Sibley pulled corn, tomatoes and dug potatoes.

The safe ran over with pies and cakes. The doctor said not to be concerned about the strange things Daddy wanted to eat. He said to give him whatever he wanted. Daddy craved hot peppers, so strangers stocked our kitchen with Tabasco sauce and red peppers.

For forty days and nights Daddy lay propped on pillows. Some days I wondered if each breath was going to be his last. There were times he didn't know day from night but if love and care could have made my daddy well, he would have lived forever.

One day the sound of crickets deafened my ears and my nose became crowded with the smell of sawdust. I couldn't stop my hands from shaking. When I saw Willie's hands shaking too, I now knew for myself how he must have been feeling all of his life. I tried to console him the way Daddy would have done. I also needed help for myself and hugged anybody not too busy to hug me back. The more I hugged the more my hands steadied.

One morning Daddy asked Monroe to bring all his children to his bedside. He beckoned for Clyde, Thelma, and me to sit on his bed despite Grandma Caroline's protests. He waved Willie, Carl, and Aaron to stand closer. Mama pulled her chair as close as she could and held John David. Between labored breaths Daddy spoke lessons.

"You children must always stay together, if not with your bodies, it must be with your spirits. Separating spirits will make as much difference to your life as mud is to blood. Willie, I want you to look after Thelma. She's too young to remember me so you must tell her about her father. Carl you should never stray too far from Clyde. Sister you and Aaron must cling to each other through thick and thin. In pairs you can rely on each other and with your spirits glued together that will keep you. Be obedient to your mother."

Daddy wet his dry, cracked lips with his tongue as he took two deep breaths. He managed a faint smile before he started speaking again.

"I'm going to be watching y'all. Remember, death won't restrain my spirit."

When Mama realized Daddy was finished and not just pausing to get a breath of air she stood up real fast holding John David on her hip.

"What about me? What about John David? You didn't say anything about me and John David!", she pleaded.

Daddy took one long lasting look at each of us but as his eyes lingered on John David, every tear he'd held back his entire life broke loose and ran down his puffy face. The last storm of his life was raging on his inside. Like rain, the tears flowed from his eyes stopping on his face giving his skin a glistening. Was this a judgment day storm, I thought? It was now near for Daddy's time and God's time to be in synchrony. This was no secret. Before he turned his face to the wall, I heard his anguished last words.

"Lord! Lord! What's going to happen to my children?"

I had to be the strong, young lady Grandma Caroline said I was, and the one Mama boasted about. I knew I had to display the strength of my father. Everybody let me.

After everyone else left I sat on the bed looking in Daddy's face trying to dismiss death from it until Monroe sent Starcie in the room to be with me. I didn't want Starcie to see him dead. That way she could help me remember the way he was, alive.

I motioned Starcie to follow me to the porch where we saw Willie. He sat with his legs dangling off the porch, his arms folded around his body like he was hugging himself. He rocked, grunted and prayed. He moaned and cried and chanted without one stutter.

"Doctor, Doctor can you tell

What will make my daddy well?

He is about to die

But I won't ever say goodbye."

He sat on the porch day after day saying the same thing until the day of the funeral when Carl, Aaron, Stephen, and Monroe forced him into getting ready. I've often wondered how long it would have been before he stopped.

The day of Daddy's funeral I wished the weather had at least matched my mood. The summer sun shouldn't have been so bright. I couldn't feel even one of its rays or any of its warmth on the inside of me. As bright as it glowed it should have lit up that deep, dark hole they were putting my Daddy in. I thought I was hearing thunder but couldn't see a cloud in the sky. Mama's wailing jolted me making me realize the thunderous sound was the dirt they were throwing on Daddy's coffin. The only comfort I got was to know that at least he's with Percy and Otsey.

Mourners slowly left the graveside. Monroe and Vee, one on each side of Mama almost had to drag her away. Willie and Malachi, Carl and Aaron, Clyde and Thelma, Walter and William with Steven walking with Starcie who was carrying John David, Aunt Martha, Aunt Ida, Uncle Stewart and Uncle Oliver and just about everybody in Franklinton departed in pairs. Rozella Robinson walked by herself.

I couldn't leave right away. It was like my feet were glued to the ground. Then, suddenly out of nowhere, a forceful wind burst forth. With the strength of a mighty hand pushing against my back, it was the kind of wind that should have been accompanied by a storm-mate but there wasn't a cloud in the sky. The wind's strength got the attention of the retreating mourners compelling them to stand still in their dusty tracks. I couldn't take my eyes off the clear blue sky still looking for a storm cloud. Whistling inside that wind blast raised such a ruckus and didn't relinquish its fervor until every flower, cross, leaf and limb on the cemetery grounds vanished from its assigned place, except one. On top of the mound of dirt on daddy's grave brighter than all the green colors of spring lay a cluster of four-leaf clovers and during my grief I found peace. I couldn't help but smile. Death wasn't winning. Joy hadn't waited to come in the morning. A loving spirit was alive.

TWENTY-TWO

Because of the sad way Mama was acting Grandma Caroline and Grandpa Frank took all of us to their house to stay for a while but Mama didn't let us stay but one day causing Grandma have to come stay at our house. I don't know how we could have made it without her. Mama began to look wasted. Her hair was falling out. Her face so thin it made her chin look more pointed and her cheeks sunken. Her grief was genuine and all consuming. She was terrified not having Daddy around. Grandma tried to persuade her.

"Marjanna enough is enough. You must eat more. You're not eating enough to keep a bird alive. And if you don't stop questioning God, you're going to bring God's wrath down on your children and yourself. God knows best. You act like you've forgotten that."

Mama cried day and night. Her sisters, Aunt Martha and Aunt Ida forced her to bathe when they came. Her hair would be so tangled, I'd had to burn hands full that came out when she'd let us comb it.

"You must accept John's death. You must see about these children. They need you. We don't mind helping but they're your responsibility and these children need you more than ever now."

Grandma pulled the covers off Mama's face and sat on the edge of the bed. There was barely enough room due to Mama being curled up on its edge with her knees almost touching her chin. Grandma started rubbing her back."

"You're pretty and you're still young. There're other men out there but they can't find you if you're lying around, hiding in here where they can't see you."

Mama motioned toward the door gesturing for Grandma to leave. Grandma didn't budge.

"There's been enough time for you to grieve. The least you can do is get back to church. Pray, Marjanna! Pray for God to give you strength."

"You told us to pray for the right husband. Martha and Ida been praying all these years and still don't have one. I prayed and thought I had the right one. Look what happened! I'm right back where I started. But I'm worse off than Martha and Ida. At least they don't have children. The husband I prayed for is gone and I'm stuck with his children. What man wants a woman with seven children?"

"There you go questioning God again and don't speak about your children that way. You're not worse off because you have children. These children are a blessing. John didn't leave you because he wanted to. The power wasn't in his hands. God doesn't make mistakes. "

"Some of the power was John's. If he hadn't started drinking, he wouldn't have gotten sick and died. Whiskey will kill anybody that drinks as much as he did everyday."

"Marjanna, a lot of men drink whiskey and don't die especially men at 33 years old. You know good and well the doctor said his heart was really bad and that's what killed him."

"He helped death along with that whiskey."

"I don't care what you say, daughter. As far as I'm concerned John Ricks had no faults."

"You're just saying that because he's dead."

"You tell me then. What other faults did you see besides as you say, he drank whiskey?"

"I'm tired of talking about John! All you want to talk about is John! John! John! John is gone. He left me with all these children. You can't argue with me about that part because it's true."

Grandma snatched her hand off Mama's back and stood up.

"Marjanna, I hope your words are coming from your grief and not your heart. John is gone whether you accept it or not. Somebody has to take care of these children whether you like it or not. It's high time you got up off your behind so you can take care of these children and yourself. You're going to have to do it whether you like it or not!"

Things were really changing while Daddy lay cooling off in the ground. For the first time I saw Grandma lose her dignified appearance and heard her raise her voice. Mama turned to face Grandma rolling her eyes. I scooted backwards afraid she was going to catch me listening.

I didn't mean to eavesdrop. Everyday I sat on the floor outside the door listening to Mama crying. I thought the way she was acting she might die too and as long as I could hear her crying I knew she was alive.

Mama didn't talk much to anybody. Just said only what was necessary. If Vee and Monroe came she told us to tell them she was sleeping. All of us children tried to talk to her when Daddy first died. She spoke to us with only a few words. Speaking Daddy's name just made her cry more so if we said it at all we whispered. If her back was turned toward the door Thelma learned to tip-toe in to play beside the bed without making a sound. One day when Mama woke up and saw Thelma she screamed so loud until Thelma was too scared to go near that room again. Thelma and

John David started whining most of the time. Carl and Aaron stayed away from the house until it was bedtime. Mama wouldn't talk to or touch any of us.

I missed Daddy like the rest of my brothers and sisters but refused to be solemn. Daddy made sure I'd found my peace in the cemetery the day he was buried. All I needed was the chance to be obedient. I wanted to honor my mother. I wanted to stay spiritually connected to my brothers and sisters like Daddy said but I couldn't feel their spirits. I couldn't feel them feeling me. We all grieved about the same thing and we all needed to feel close to someone with a connection to Daddy. That someone was Mama and she was disconnected from everybody.

Mama's actions made me think a lot about the day Daddy kept her from slapping me. Her hand would have hurt but not as bad as now with her not touching me at all. Whether it was Grandma, Aunt Ida or Aunt Martha combing my hair, I didn't care. I'd close my eyes and pretend I was feeling Mama's hands. I craved love from somebody Daddy had loved as much as he loved us. What made me the saddest was hearing Mama say she wish she didn't have us. I couldn't for the life of me understand why she questioned God. All of that made me think too about what was going to happen to us when Grandma Caroline went home. Grandma kept busy and kept us busy. She never acted like she was going to give up on making Mama well again. Eventually she found just the right thing to say to get Mama's attention.

"Pastor told me they're going to need a teacher over in Bolivar at Jones Chapel School. Their teacher has gotten too old. He asked whether you might be interested in the job. Said he sees how well you've done with your children. All you have to do is say you want the job"

I thought Grandma must be losing her mind and tried to peep in the room. I wanted to look at Mama. The idea of work, I didn't think, ever crossed Mama's mind. She told Clyde and me never to let it cross ours. Said women were supposed to be taken care of by men like Daddy, Grandpa Frank, and Monroe Blackburn. She said women were to leave their father's house with their hands untouched by outside work. Said she felt sorry for women that didn't have a man to support them. On the other hand, she had respect for Rozella Robinson, the only teacher in Franklinton who, because she was the only teacher, had overcome stigmas and ridicule and earned the respect of everyone.

In those days, teachers couldn't be married much less have children. Mama wasn't exactly married, and she wasn't exactly single either. She had seven children and had buried a husband. Maybe she was being given the chance no one else had been given. Maybe she could give honor to the word, work, for a woman with children and no husband.

Grandma must have been on to something. Mama's hand suddenly moved off the bald spot she'd made from constantly rubbing her head when she was annoyed. She sat straight up, throwing her legs over the side of the bed. I could see a little glimmer in her usually dull, swollen eyes with the dark circles. I was so excited that I leaned in too far bumping my head on the half-way opened door. Mama saw me before Grandma.

"My goodness, Sister! How long have you been sitting there?"

Grandma walked over-reaching for my trembling hands and pulled me up.

Mama reached around Grandma gathering me in her arms.

"My Goodness, Sister! Your eyes look just like your father's!"

Mama started to cry again.

"Oh Sister! Don't let me lose you too!"

I thought Mama was delusional until I wriggled my head out of her tight grip and ran to the mirror. My eyes were puffy and red just like Daddy's had been. I must have been crying without even realizing it. Mama must have thought I was dying too.

"Please forgive me! I'm sorry. I'll make it up to you. All of us together can make it."

I don't know how long Mama held me that day and I don't know whether it was her or me trembling.

TWENTY-THREE

Nothing around me looked or felt like I thought it was supposed to. My feeling that way made me pay closer attention to changing colors in the sky. I listened to words in birds' songs and smelled sweet fragrances of night. The only way I could tell fall was coming was the way Louisiana humidity didn't take my breath away. The sun had moved further south and the days were getting shorter. It was time for green leaves to fade into golden and brown hues the morning Mama and I started on the first of our many walks into the town of Bolivar to Jones Chapel School. Willie and Malachi brought us as close as they could before turning around to go back and not be late for school at Crystal Springs School.

Mama had changed for the better once she found out she was going to be a teacher. She was filled with a mixture of melancholy and excitement but still worried about making it on her own. She'd never even had to try. I helped at home as much as she'd let me. I didn't mind but Grandma said I was only a child and should have been doing little girl things instead of so much work around the house. I was so glad Mama was being my mother again. She wanted me close to her most of the time saying the older I got the more I looked just like my daddy. I guess I was the greatest reminder she had of his face.

Once Mama got out of bed and started talking, she expressed all of her concerns over and over to anyone that listened. She talked about how much responsibility it was to teach others' children. She wanted so much to do her very best teaching, but it was more for praise than for the love of the job. We didn't need the money. Daddy left enough for us never to want for anything. Money wasn't enough. Mama worried about whether the parents of the school children accepted her, a woman once married with almost as many children at home as was going to be in the class. She needed their love to become one of those name-branded people.

Mama and I went everywhere and did most things together. She even let me choose dresses that were more grown-up than Clyde's. Blue gingham ribbons in my hair matched the blue gingham dress I'd chosen especially for our first day at Jones Chapel School. She said making a good impression on the first day was important.

Mama was grateful to Vee for offering to take care of Thelma and John David when school started. She asked that Monroe and Vee talk about Daddy as much as they could because the children were too young to remember him. John David was only six months old and Thelma only two years when Daddy died. When Mama spoke about Thelma and John David being too young to remember she always rubbed her hand across her chest while repeating one of those old Louisiana isms. She said a child who would never know his father could rub your pain away.

Instead of questioning, now Mama thanked God all the time for letting her have Daddy even if for just a little while. She thought Daddy must have known his life was going to be short because of how well he'd trained my brothers to take on the role of men, as young as they were. They did Daddy's usual chores and were good at handling them.

Carl and Aaron wanted to return to Crystal Springs School so they could stay closer to home. Willie didn't want to return to school at all.

Mama and Monroe had a time with him. They had to go slow and ease up to him a little at a time. Monroe said Willie and Malachi had a lot of recovering to do.

At first Willie didn't talk to any of us. He just kept on saying that poem. Malachi didn't act any better either but his started from the day Daddy got sick. Monroe told Mama to leave both of them to their grief. Folks thought Willie lost his mind and Malachi too. That big, ole, black stallion had to be roped and tied to keep him out of the house. If Willie hadn't stayed with him, he would have butted his head to pieces. After Daddy's funeral Willie led Malachi to the woods where he'd sit on Daddy's tree stump. He was so busy crying, rocking and saying that poem that he wasn't watching when Malachi ran away. Men found him digging with all the strength in his hoof, uncovering the dirt from Daddy's grave. Those men said that horse was missing Daddy and hurting too bad and needed to be put out of his misery. They would have killed him if somebody hadn't run to get Monroe.

"Not so fast!" Monroe told them.

It took several men to corral that wild acting horse. Willie still sitting on the tree stump heard the wagon rolling by and recognized Malachi's consistent, distressed squeal. He saw Malachi bound up like a wild buck. That was the first time that poem stopped spewing from Willie's mouth. He grabbed his knife and cut those ropes as he whispered words to that horse. He'd pause and listen like someone was whispering to him what he was to say. Malachi became calm and listened. After that, on another day I heard him tell Malachi he had orders not to leave until they both felt better. He didn't leave him either. Slept right there on the ground in the barn.

Just like Daddy he took Malachi everywhere he went. They went to the cemetery almost every day. Sometimes they'd both lay on top of and by Daddy's grave. The only time I didn't leave flowers was when I'd see them there. After all, that was the only peaceful place they both knew, and I didn't want to disturb them. Willie stroked Malachi's mane and Malachi licked Willie's hair. One became better while taking care of the other.

Mama was thinking about all of that the first morning we walked to Jones Chapel School. She held my hand and kept looking over me and herself. I was watching other children walking in front and behind us. One mother carried a baby about the age of John David as she walked with her other school-age children. It made me think about Mama's worrying that Daddy in his dying wishes didn't give John David a partner. Mama dismissed thinking that there was no one to pair John David with. After all, seven is an uneven number.

The closer we got to the school the more people we saw walking in the same direction. Mama squeezed my hand, pulling me backwards sort of like the way one slows a horse's gait. She wanted all the people to get in front of us.

My goodness! I thought. I couldn't believe the sight in front of us when the school came into view. The school porch was covered with children and their parents cheering and waving us forward. Some hands held brightly wrapped presents for Mama. With one deep breath her nervousness flew away. I could feel her hand relax on mine. It was beginning to feel like that dreadful summer was over. The sight of a new season for us was being born on a school porch directly in front of us. We were arriving at our new life. The late summer sunlight blinded me appearing just as it was supposed to.

TWENTY-FOUR

Mama let me help with the children almost everyday. I read them stories. I assisted Mama teaching them to read and write. I recited poems and taught them church songs. When we could be outside, the children and I taught each other games and dances. I was satisfied. Jones Chapel School was good for me while it lasted.

Mama's elation was short-lived. She discarded her excitement for teaching faster than she discarded all those new clothes she had made and bought us. She developed an obsession for us having new dresses and shoes which took the place of everything that made her come to Jones Chapel School. Even the briskness in her walk faded faster than it took her to open all those gifts the parents brought. Grandma thought it was the long walk we took everyday that was causing her to be exhausted, so Willie and Monroe took turns taking us all the way. That didn't help. Becoming an important person in Bolivar wasn't working for Mama. Parents wanted smart children. After their Grande welcome, they wanted smart children and focused their minds on that and not on Mama and me wearing new dresses and shoes every time you looked around. Mama started to complain that there weren't enough of the right kind of people for her in Bolivar. What I think she meant was there weren't any men in Bolivar paying her any attention and neither were the women in the way she wanted them to. Grandma said she could see Mama slowly slipping backwards where she was after Daddy died.

One day Grandma Caroline sent Mama's brother, Uncle Stewart Cryer to talk to his sister. Uncle Stewart sat in Daddy's chair that was made especially for a big man. It fit Uncle Stewart very well. He sat comfortably watching Mama from his clear, light, brown eyes as she ironed and hoping that what he was about to say didn't annoy her.

"Marjanna, I need you to think about what I'm going to say. Mama, Daddy and I think you and the children should move closer to me. Change would be good for all of you. You all being near me could help me too. Those boys are getting older and bigger and need a man around them. Helping you with them gives me something to do. When they really start acting like grown men you won't be able to handle them. Daddy's getting old and Monroe has his own family to see about."

Mama wouldn't look at Uncle Stewart, but I knew she was listening. She ironed the same sleeve over and over again. That was going to be the most perfectly ironed sleeve in Franklinton. Every now and then she wiped her forehead with the back of her hand.

"Greensburg is a nice town. I know you and the children would just love Lambert Chapel Church. The congregation is small, but the warmth and friendliness of the people make up for it. If you lived there the boys could go to work with me when they're ready. I can get jobs for them on the railroad."

Uncle Stewart was talking so fast I thought he was trying to say everything all in one sentence. He thought it was going to be difficult to convince Mama, so he acted like he had to say everything all at once. I was surprised to hear him talking so much. Usually he displayed the kind of quietness that was like Grandma Caroline.

Uncle Stewart was the oldest of Mama's sisters and brothers and the first to leave home. He was also the first colored man in Washington Parish to work in a high paying job on the railroad. Grandpa Frank let Uncle Stewart think he got the job on his own. Washington Parish was full of strangers coming to town to hire railroad men. Grandpa knew there must be one sucker among the so-called, smart strangers. Their pockets were lined with plenty of cash and Grandpa Frank's plan was to get all those fat pockets lined in a row and get some of that money thrown in his direction.

One night, grandpa won everybody's stash including the one belonging to the railroad foreman who was supposedly the smartest among them. The foreman asked Grandpa for a loan to try to win some of his money back. Grandpa bargained, making an offer to the foreman that was worth more than cash. The man agreed to give one of my uncles a job with the railroad if he lost. Grandpa was on a winning streak. The man lost, gave the job to Uncle Stewart and Grandpa gave the foreman his money back.

Uncle Stewart was pleased to take the job and wasn't the least bit sorry to leave Franklinton. He stayed as long as he could to help Grandma when Grandpa lost gambling heavy. Uncle Stewart had long-since given up hope trying to reform Grandpa and didn't want to live at home any longer. After a lot of praying, Uncle Stewart, with God's help, made a decision that Grandma was the one that needed to put her foot down on Grandpa's bad habit.

It was a wonder that as handsome as Uncle Stewart was, big and tall with curly, graying temples, some cagey Louisiana woman hadn't captured him. Monroe and Vee teased him about being thirty-seven years old and still single. He answered them saying he was still looking. Said he didn't want a woman as passive as Grandma who didn't chastise Grandpa for gambling or a woman as fickle as Mama or women as stuck up as Aunt Martha and Aunt Ida.

"I don't know if there's a teaching job in Greensburg or not. It doesn't matter. I have enough to help you if you need it."

Well! That statement stopped the over-ironing of that shirt sleeve.

"I will have you to know, Stewart Cryer that John Ricks didn't leave me destitute and I have money saved from my teaching job. If push comes to shove, the boys can work but right now it isn't necessary that we take charity."

"See there you go. MY NAME is not charity. I was just making you an offer. Besides, boys need to have a job just because they're boys. They need their own money for themselves. They've outgrown little boys selling brooms. Haven't you noticed how they're changing right before your very eyes? They're changing into men. If you go ahead and sell this shanty and the land, you'll have enough to live the rest of your life."

Mama looked up again, her piercing eyes going straight into Uncle Stewart's.

"DON'T YOU DARE CALL MY HOUSE A SHANTY! JOHN WOULD NEVER HAVE US LIVE IN A SHANTY."

"Marjanna, don't get so upset. I call anywhere that anybody lives in Louisiana, a shanty. You know as well as I that shanty is a Louisiana word."

Mama stopped ironing and took a seat next to Uncle Stewart in Willie's chair. Her face showed her pondering at the same time she spoke.

"I don't know a soul in St. Helena Parish."

"So what? I didn't know anyone either. You can get to know new people like I did. They're just people like us. Think it over." I discerned serious thoughts in Mama's face, and it didn't take many days for her to start talking it over with us. I was the first one she spoke to about it. I didn't want to go and told her so. Greenburg was too far from Grandma Caroline, Starcie, Steven, Walter and William, Crystal Springs Church, Percy, Otsey and Daddy. Especially Steven!

Mama easily convinced the others, reminding them of places Daddy told us about. She said we'd be living closer to New Orleans and going to Mardi Gras would be easier if we wanted to go. She reminded them of the beautiful, glittering costumes and the masks everybody wore. She intrigued them with stories of mysteries, telling how revelers committed heinous crimes while hiding their identities behind those beautiful masks, not easily being caught. She created a longing in my sisters and brothers to experience those things Daddy had told us about but left us too soon to show us. They believed that one day we'd be a part of the fun and frolic, marching in a magnificent parade. They liked the idea of being close to Uncle Stewart and in a new place. They wanted to leave their pain behind and I was out-numbered in the vote. I was consoled only after Mama said I could come back to see Grandma Caroline as often as I wanted.

I found out that it didn't really matter what any of the rest of us wanted. Mama's mind was made up. I heard her tell Vee how her chances of finding another husband had to be greater in Greensburg than in Franklinton.

TWENTY-FIVE

The Blackburn family sadly did their part in helping to get us ready to leave the only home any of us except Mama knew. Vee and Starcie didn't stop sewing until they made each of us our own quilt and enough doilies to fill a room. The quilt that Starcie made for me had both our names sewn together in the middle. I knitted Starcie a blue afghan with our names together and carved a heart for Steven with the two of our initials. My brothers carved wooden horses for Walter, William and Steven engraved with Malachi's name.

Mama's promise made to Monroe one time that she'd send for him if she needed him wasn't enough. He asked her to make the promise over and over. Monroe wanted to be sure he could keep a promise he and Daddy made years before in the woods by a tree stump that they would take care of each others' families if anything happened to one or the other. He told Mama how all she had to do was get a word to him and he'd drop everything to come. I wondered how he could keep his promise when we were going to be so far away. How was he going to know when we needed him? Some of the questions I had were not so good and the day we were leaving I felt the same way I did when we were leaving Crystal Springs A.M.E. Church, that day our picnic was ruined.

The Blackburns trailed us as far as they could. They had come so far that I thought and secretly wished, they were going all the way. The ride didn't feel rugged until I turned around and saw the Blackburns turning around to go back. Willie and Carl stopped both wagons when I screamed. Horses and wagons on both ends of the road stood still until I couldn't cry anymore.

TWENTY-SIX

The ride wasn't comfortable for any of us. There was very little room for sitting. Mama didn't leave anything that she thought would erase a memory. She even hoarded broken things in boxes. The two wagons were so tight we took turns walking part of the way. I didn't want to go to Greensburg but was so glad when we got there.

We didn't stay at Uncle Stewart's house long enough to unpack. Mama quickly found a house in town in walking distance of the church. We'd never lived in a town, especially in the heart of it. Mama said we could meet new people faster if we didn't have to travel so far to where they were. She said we'd soon have people inside and outside the town coming to us. She could hardly wait to have a look at the school and Lambert Chapel A.M.E. Church where Uncle Stewart attended. My seeing that church was the first thing in Greenburg to make me sad.

Lambert Chapel Church: Now that was a shanty if ever, I'd seen one. It didn't hold a candle to Crystal Springs Church. It was no bigger than a shot gun house. There was no organ and the old, rickety, out of tune piano with missing keys and peeling paint sat isolated in a corner. They didn't even have a choir. I wouldn't have buried an animal in that over-grown, dead tree cemetery. There wasn't a flower or cross in sight. If any were there, you couldn't find them for the weeds.

Lambert Chapel Church ran over with faults. Mama's mind ran over with ideas and opportunities and at our first church meeting she announced loudly to the people that she was going to donate a brand, new piano. She announced quietly to the minister and deacons that it would be given on the condition that I could play in the service as often as I wanted. They didn't refuse the offer. Then she challenged me to be in charge of straightening out that mess of a cemetery. I didn't need much persuasion. I missed being near Daddy and my little brothers and it had been too long since my hands had touched God's rich, precious soil. I needed to see colors coming out of the ground again and had to muddle through all of that untidiness so I could find four-leaf clovers.

Mama recruited Carl and Aaron with Willie in charge to start building new pews. First, they knocked out walls to make more room. Uncle Stewart came to help. Soon others joined in and together we made our church stand out from all the others. Membership grew rapidly. It seemed like people wanted their faith to be tidy. Some came just to see but stayed only because they'd heard about the brand, new piano. Speaking about thriving, Mama was proud of all of her accomplishments. We even liked our teacher and all of us did well in school.

Mama and I started sharing everything about our life. We drew strength from each other. I caught her looking in my eyes a lot. They reminded her of Daddy. She hugged all of us more. Thelma stopped whining. Mama began to run John David's hand across her chest, I guess to try to rub away what was left of her pain. John David was growing and getting into everything. Clyde loved to read. She didn't care so much about shopping as long as we bought her a book. Sometimes, Willie went with Uncle Stewart to work on the railroad. Carl and Aaron were hired by the towns' people to do odd jobs after school. The best times for me was when Mama was teaching me to cook, sew better, braid hair and to learn all things little girls need to be taught by their mothers. Mama praised me a lot. Our time together made me not miss Grandma Caroline so much. I still missed Daddy though. He would have let me help build those pews but, THANK GOODNESS anyway, that none of us looked sad anymore.

Mama started boasting about us again. She looked very well. She bought the best fabric to make her clothes. The lace she sewed around her collars and cuffs cost more than some paid for a whole dress. The bald spot she had rubbed in her head was almost covered with hair. She was eating all that was in front of her giving roundness to her hips. She was feeling and looking much better, but I didn't like to see her putting too much rouge on her cheeks and so much blaringly, red lipstick that made her lips look like they were bleeding.

Mama studied the faces of all who entered the church doors and all the new faces in town. Nothing brought her the satisfaction she wanted in finding the man she constantly searched for. She found out, the men in Greensburg were no different from the ones in Franklinton. They were either married, not educated enough for her taste or just plain not interested in her. She was lonely for a man to the point of desperation. She ignored, at first, Will Johnson's clandestine winks. I watched his eyes follow her as she busily moved all over the place. I'd already heard that Will was a married man and I didn't trust him the first time I watched him lay his eyes on Mama.

"Why does Mr. Johnson keep on flirting with you? Do you like him?"

"I don't really think he means anything by it, Sister. He's probably just trying to be friendly."

"I hope that's all he's doing because he has a wife and I heard some children too."

"I don't think he has a wife. He used to be married just as I was but he's not anymore. I think it is true that he has children."

"How do you know he isn't married? Have you talked to him?"

"I didn't talk to him but heard others talking about him. They say he's one of the best cobblers around. They say he can really make a shoe!"

"I bet he does have a wife. He looks too sneaky. I bet he's a liar."

"Watch your mouth, girl!"

Mama looked uncomfortable. The last time she spoke to me in that tone was the time Daddy grabbed her hand just in time to stop her from hitting me. I obeyed and closed my mouth, but she couldn't make me close my mind.

Will Johnson had told the people of Greensburg how he'd love to have a church of his own to run. He wasn't choosey either. Any church, any denomination, would do. Some folks with tongue in cheek called Will Johnson, "Preacher". I heard Daddy say preachers had to be called to the ministry. The voice calling Will Johnson was coming from his wallet.

A preacher was one of the few independent jobs a colored man could have. They weren't completely safe from the wrath of white men but weren't abused as often or as harshly. Preachers wore fine clothes, lived in better houses and could spend as much money as they wanted without white people's questions.

I heard grown-ups saying how Will wanted to take over the ministry at the newly renovated Lambert Chapel Church. They said he went town to one town in Louisiana but failed to be able to start his own church. He'd take Lambert chapel if he could get it. I heard a lady warn Mama to be careful about believing words she was going to hear coming from Will Johnson's mouth. She told Mama how Will told lies to stir up dissension among Lambert Chapel members. The minister, at the time, came from another parish but for only one or two Sundays a month which made it difficult for him to keep up with all the church gossip. Will accused the preacher of having affairs with many of the women in town. He accused the deacons of stealing from the Sunday offering. He offered to replace the stolen money with money from his own pockets. The church wanted high rollers like Will Johnson and prayerfully accepted his money offer as well as his pockets full of lies.

Will Johnson was a whole foot shorter than Mama. He had tiny eyes that looked crossed if he'd let you stare long enough. His yellow teeth, too large for his mouth, hung over his bottom lip and drew attention to his crooked nose that appeared to have been distorted with a fist. Worry lines around his mouth and eyes blended with the keloid scars on his right cheek and left ear. His speech and mannerisms showed a man trying hard to be confident but not knowing just how. Flashing his money and buying everything including friendship and trust made him attractive to many.

Another name for Will was Shoe Man. No matter how damaged a shoe, he could repair it to make it look new. In those different towns where he'd travel, he'd also set up shops, repairing boots and shoes. Some boots and shoes had sentimental value in their soles. Those he repaired and renewed for grateful, rich white patrons made some of his work qualify as heirlooms. Those patrons respected his craftsmanship and were generous. Will's remarkable skills made him remarkable money.

Those skills as a cobbler gave Will the freedom from hard, physical labor most others had to endure. Some hated to see in him the success they didn't possess in themselves. Poor, uneducated white men thought the color of Will's money didn't match the color of his skin. To them, no colored man was supposed to make that kind of money. For colored men, Will represented all that they wanted but couldn't achieve. Hatred came from both sides. Will did his part in helping to bring it on. It wasn't necessary but he boasted about his extraordinary abilities to "make a shoe"! Everybody already knew that. He flashed rolls of money and pulled his gold watch from his pocket to show it off too many times. He sought out certain kinds of women, single or married, searched for their vulnerabilities and delved right in, learning and taking advantage of their weaknesses. What he was able to give them was far more than they had or had ever been given. They loved his money, his frivolous gifts, his independence, and his title as a preacher.

In some of the places where he traveled, Will was threatened, and robbed. White women were encouraged by their men to lie about Will and say things like he'd made passes at them. Such lies often kept Will running and hiding. Jealous, colored men and rejected, colored women told where he hid out. He was often hunted and chased like a hungry dog chasing a rabbit.

On the way to Greenburg, Will stayed in one town long enough to marry and have children. The family went with him everywhere and eventually to Greensburg. Having a family made Will appear respectable and changed the description that made him attract the wrong kind of attention, but it didn't change his desire to deceive. Will Johnson couldn't fool all the people of Lambert Chapel Church, so he'd do the next best thing. He'd fool the one who held the church in the palms of both her hands. Will read Mama like a book. Mama was watching him too, but she couldn't see straight. He could.

Will noticed how Mama craved someone praising her. He made comments about her pretty, red lips and gave her compliments on the way she dressed. At first, she resisted, but, barely. After a while I noticed her not resisting at all. Her glances became less disapproving and her smiles converted more favorably toward Will's flirtatious gestures.

Will Johnson's skill as a shoe man was the only thing that made him what he thought to be an important man. He was an ill-bred egotist and a wannabe who didn't really fit too comfortably anywhere. He didn't have the kind of in-bred pride like my daddy. Daddy's self-esteem let him stand toe to toe with anybody and look them square in the eyes. Will Johnson's head was mostly slightly bowed or hung to one side. His eyes couldn't stand the light in another's. The gold my daddy inherited was worth more than both his and Will Johnson's weights and Daddy hardly told anyone about it with a voice that was soft spoken and gentle. Will Johnson boasted loudly to anybody he met about the budges in his pocket. He was boisterous, boastful, and loud and could read very little.

Mama's standards for what she wanted in a man had been set long before she met Daddy. I wondered how she could even think about spending time with a married man and with one so unlike my daddy. I guess having the attention of Will Johnson was better than not having any attention at all. Before she went too far, I told Uncle Stewart so he could see exactly what was going on.

At first, she didn't give Uncle Stewart an answer when he asked her about it.

"Marjanna, you need to be careful about what you're doing. It's so easy for one bad move to lead to a disaster."

When Mama couldn't think of words for a good argument, she'd press her lips together, turn her head and was the best I've seen at ignoring somebody.

Mama didn't know whether Will Johnson was even his real name. Despite the whispered gossip, she believed anything he told her. He told her he didn't live with his wife and children. I knew that wasn't the truth and thought Mama knew it too. Will persisted in his pursuit and Mama submitted.

When Will was sure he had won Mama over, he was so cruel to his wife she ran away leaving all five of their children behind. Will took up most of Mama's time after that. He courted her heavily, bringing her redder lipstick, cheap perfume and grandiose ideas about the future they could have together. Mama started buying him gifts too. She bought him expensive hats, bottles of strong whiskey and when she did come home from his house, she fed him like he was the one providing the food.

I was never lonely before Daddy died and couldn't imagine being as lonely as I felt when he first left. But here it was again. I was losing Mama who had become my best friend. This time the loneliness was because of Will Johnson.

TWENTY-SEVEN

The changes between Mama and me came too soon. We no longer talked and shared everything. She shopped with Will now and not with me anymore. All the other things I'd been taught by her, Grandma Caroline, and Vee and most of the chores became my duties all by myself. Daddy must have known when he was building that stool for me that I'd need it sooner than I thought. I had to stand on it to reach the top of the stove to cook. I also needed it to climb on the counter to reach the top of the cupboard. Clyde tried to help but Thelma and John David needed her too. At times they cried for me. That made my day even busier.

Being without my daddy and my missing him and us walking together, talking together and enjoying and sharing whatever there was to see was difficult but Mama had started us doing those things again, making us as close as a family should be. I remembered the togetherness as one of the most favorite of my things that Mama snatched away. Her giving us all that good love and attention then suddenly snatching it all away made me sad and started me grieving for Daddy all over again.

One Sunday after church Mama asked us to walk home without her. We had never done that. Before that day, I hadn't had a heavy, cloudy day feeling since we left Franklinton. What I felt in the pit of my stomach was identical to the feeling I had the day Mama came to school and gave Rozella Robinson permission to beat me. I knew this Sunday had something to do with the storm of 1907 and how the storm that was coming was going to be as disastrous as any that God had sent.

I functioned on very little energy, hardly able to make one foot move in front of the other. I tried my best to focus on the good times, but those notions of a dim prediction overshadowed my thoughts. It was like my energy had been sucked right out of me like a tornado sucks up and destroys everything in its path.

I waited for Mama as long as I could before I served dinner hoping she would soon be home. I thought I'd feel better just seeing her face. We ate late and I finished my chores functioning more from habits than from consciousness. Later, I couldn't even remember the motions of my body. I just knew all the chores were done. I do remember dragging myself to the porch, sitting on the swing, swinging, and singing every song that I knew. I wondered if I was feeling what Uncle David had felt the night he had sat on his porch singing while waiting for the coming of that torrential storm that was filled with wrath. Near sunset, the inevitable tragedy began to unfold.

Shadows of tree branches swayed on the ground with the evening breeze. Flickering red and gold streaks of the dying sunlight convulsed in my eyes. That summer day I wished my eyes to focus on darkness the rest of my life rather than have them behold what came into my sight.

In the waning daylight shadows, Will appeared first, leading his horse and Mama down the road. I came to my senses just in time to jump off the porch and grab John David's hand to keep him from running to meet her and saving him from getting his little feelings hurt. It was clear to me that Mama didn't see anything else around her. Her head was hung down with her eyes fixed upward on Will.

The day Daddy died a river of tears flowed down his swollen face from his swollen eyes. That Sunday, just before sunset, I knew the reason he had cried. Daddy knew a lonely heart and a broken heart makes for a reckless heart. He was describing Mama's heart and he had said with his last breaths, "Lord, what is going to happen to my children?"

I took the longest, deepest breaths that I could so I wouldn't vomit.

TWENTY-EIGHT

Like the rest of us, Uncle Stewart was worried and never stopped trying to head off trouble.

"Marjanna, have you taken a serious look at what you're getting yourself into? Why would you want to settle for somebody that's a no body like Will Johnson? You don't even pretend to know anything about him. And then, for him to ask you to bring your children to live in HIS house is a doggone shame. There're already too many people living in that house and they're grown folks, compared to the ages of your children. Grown folks should live in their own house. Have you thought about what might happen to your children?"

"You don't know what you're talking about and I'm not going to let anything happen to my children."

"You don't always LET things happen to children. Right now, your head is so wrapped up in Will until all you can think about now is yourself. You haven't considered what these children might have to endure."

"I've already endured a lot all by myself or haven't you noticed. I've been too lonely, too long without a man."

"Don't be unreasonable, Marjanna. You have it made a whole lot better than a lot of women, married or not. And I guess you don't count the things Monroe and I have done for you."

"There are some things that would be sinful for you and Monroe to do?"

"Well I guess I'll hush my mouth on that. But you don't have to settle for any, ole, just a piece of a man like Will Johnson just so you'll have a man. Will talked you into marrying him and since you're so determined, just don't put these children where, what others care about them won't amount to a hill of beans. All of Will's children are just about grown. Yours are not. No real man would let you do that to your children. I can't imagine all those grown folks telling your children what to do. You need to get some sense in your head, girl!"

"What makes you think I don't have good sense? I got me a man, didn't I?"

"You call that a man?", Uncle Stewart mumbled under his breath. "Let the boys come stay with me, then."

"Will and I already talked about that. He wants us all to be together. Everybody is going with me."

"Well, I'm going to come and get them at the first sign of trouble and, mark my word, there's going to be trouble. You could avoid all this. The children shouldn't have to go to live there. You can take care of yourself. Your children still need to be protected from that kind of riffraff over there."

"Don't you dare call Will's family bad names. You don't even know them, much less to call them riffraff! Stay out of my business and take care of your own. Such as it is. I'm making a life for myself. You should be making one of your own instead of putting your nose in mine."

"MYSELF! MYSELF! See there! You're only thinking about yourself. That's what I mean. Give some of your thoughts to your children. What kind of life are you making for them? When the mess starts, remember I asked you that question?"

Uncle Stewart looked burdened. I know he was thinking about Grandma Caroline telling him to take care of us, but he couldn't do it and it wasn't his fault. Mama just wouldn't listen. She didn't give anything he said a second thought. She was trying too hard, working too fast, seeing how quickly she could get everything and us ready to move in with her new husband and his children.

TWENTY-NINE

Every space in Will Johnson's house had a live body in it at bedtime. Willie, Carl and Aaron were ordered to sleep on the porch with Will's sons, Leon and David. Will's daughters, Emma, Mary and Hattie Mae shared a room in the back of the house, off the kitchen. At least the daughters, Will and Mama had a bed. Clyde and I slept on the floor just beneath the sofa where Thelma and John David tossed and turned from a lack of comfortable space.

At mealtime, the most chaotic time of the day was when I'd often lose my appetite. Gluttony from a diet of too much fat showed in Will's children's big bellies and bodies. They acted as if they'd never heard of good manners. When Mama unpacked her fine, linen napkins and placed them on the table, they acted like they didn't know what to do with them. Leon and David used them to blow their noses or wipe their brows. Emma, Mary and Hattie Mae left them in their place unless they used them to spit out bones or food. If one of us found a seat at the table, which was rare, they laughed at us or turned their noses up at us when we used them the proper way. At mealtime, we sat on the floor or any place we could with our plates on our laps.

It wasn't long before I found out what it must have felt like for slave children Daddy had told me about. Those big, fat, snuff dipping, lazy daughters of Will had never done much work in their lives. I was required to do Will's children's share along with mine and Mama's share of chores. I didn't mind too much so we could have some measure of comfort.

One day I was standing on one end of the back porch busy with the ironing. Mama and Will sat, rocking at the opposite end. I watched from the corners of my eyes, with Will watching me from the corners of his sneaky eyes. His eyes weren't just supervising my work. Those eyes were making plans. A brown stain formed on the edge of the porch when he spit his tobacco juice out. He wiped the excess from his mouth, leaned backwards, straining the back of his rocker and turned toward Mama.

"Marjanna, That sho is a smart little, ole gal you got yourself. Can you teach my girls to clean, cook and iron as good as she can.? They need to know how."

"Yes, I can. I'm the one that taught Sister."

"First there's something else you need to help me do. I want you to help me get myself a church of my own to run so you can be a preacher's wife. Preacher's wives ain't supposed to work. When my daughters get through learning, they can do the work around the house. I can use Sister to do something else."

"What do you need her to do? She can do anything."

"I got big plans. I want to build my own church. It's taking too long for those folks at Lambert Chapel to make up their mind. Ain't gonna give them any more money. You see, if I could get me a good crop of cotton going, I can soon have enough to build my own church. I've always had my shoe business and ain't never had to work for white folks. Seems like the shoe business makes me good money but keeps me in trouble. I gotta start making plans for something else. A preacher is the only kind of colored man white folks won't bother too much. Some of 'em act like they scared of our God."

I heard Will sucking his teeth. When I glanced at him again, he had started picking between his teeth with a straw. I didn't understand how Mama could stand him. His tobacco-stained, buck teeth didn't look like they'd ever been cleaned.

"My other wife didn't know too much about anything outside the cotton field to teach my girls. If they learn the lady-like stuff you know, they'll act like a preacher's children and they can stay at the house and work. Leon and David and your sons can work together to make us a good cotton crop. Sister and Clyde both big enough to go to the cotton field and carry their share of the load."

Mama rocked and twisted her plait.

"My girls have never had to do field work. The most Sister and Clyde ever did outside the house was take care of the vegetable garden and their flower beds. Their father would never have allowed it."

"Well Marjanna, that just boils down to them being too spoiled. They need to learn what hard work is. Hard work ain't never killed nobody. We need to prepare for whatever comes along. They need to prepare too."

Will sucked his teeth, dropped the straw, and sucked his teeth again.

"Listen to me good 'cause I ain't gonna say this but one time. I'm your husband now. Your other one died. Let's leave him dead. Don't ever bring his name or anything else about him to me again. I'm your children's daddy now. From this day on they'll take my name. Just like my name's Johnson, your name's Johnson, their name's gonna be Johnson too."

Mama dropped her head.

"Yes Will. The Bible speaks of a woman obeying her husband. Tell me what you want us to do and I'll see that it's done."

I dropped the iron. Will's shirt slid off the ironing board, blowing into the yard. When Mama and Will looked up at me, I was rolling my eyes. I walked in the house and slammed the door as forcefully and loudly as I could make it sound. Will jumped to his feet. I could hear his startled response.

"Aint no sense in nobody being that disrespectful. You can see it for yourself. That gal needs some discipline and I got just the kind she needs."

Will squeezed Mama's hand as she bowed her head again.

THIRTY

With my head hung down all the time, cotton plants were all that swept across my pupils. After Uncle Stewart took Willie, Carl, and Aaron with him to work on the railroad I didn't want to look up and down that road all the time just to see it empty. I had watched for my brothers day after day when they first left but with each sunset my heart gathered more weight. I was scared to look for them anymore for fear of my heart breaking into pieces like Daddy's. The only reason I lifted my head that day was because I heard Malachi's frantic bray.

Echoes of the sound of Malachi came from the direction of the house. I ran close enough to see that Will had hitched Malachi to a plow, but Malachi didn't budge as Will's anger snapped out of that whip he used to beat the horse. Malachi's bray was pleading from the pain of those forceful licks. I didn't understand how that horse could stand still the way Will was beating him. Will finally gave up, unhitched Malachi, and tried to climb on his back. Malachi lay down then suddenly stood, bucking, and turning until he threw Will off. Will screamed, calling our horse a son-of-a-bitch. Malachi started running for his dear life. My sprinting legs came through cotton rows as fast as that strong, spring-time wind. I chased and called out his name. The sound of my voice, my puffing and panting competing with the sound of rustling trees and the strong breeze was like a whisper. Malachi was old but ran like a buck.

I was unable to keep running against the wind. My breathing became more and shallow with each forceful stride and pushed against my tightening chest. My last conscious memory was leaning against the silo watching spilled grain fade in and out of my sight, changing from large to small particles until the entire scene vanished. The next thing I remember was a tug and something cold on my face. My fear, my splitting headache and the sickness in my stomach wouldn't let me open my eyes right away. Becoming more alert made me know that it was Malachi tugging at my dress and licking the sweat off my face. With all that fog in my brain, I couldn't tell how long I'd been unconscious but just knowing Malachi was with me, I felt safe.

Malachi lay down so I could climb on his back. He carried me straight to Uncle Stewart's house where I think he was headed in the first place. I wanted to rest and wait for Uncle Stewart so I could tell him what happened but changed my mind when my thoughts went to Clyde, Thelma, and John David. I also knew getting back wasn't going to be good for me. I knew Mama and Will were waiting to fuss at me.

Mama was nowhere in sight when I got back but Will was standing in the field waiting with his arms behind his back. I could tell he was holding something. He started walking forward toward me.

"Where you been, gal?"

He didn't wait for an answer. The next thing I felt was the sting of his razor strap so forceful until I fell to the ground. After that first lick, I looked up in time to see his arm rising above his head. I dropped my head in time to see him rising on his toes. The licks made me know how Malachi must have felt. He spoke as that strap tore into me.

"You been somewhere hiding, trying to get out of work?"

I could feel my flesh being pulled apart. He had already scarred my heart. Now he was trying to mar my body for life.

"Please don't hit me again?"

"SHUT UP. DON'T YOU EVER LEAVE OUT OF THIS FIELD UNTIL ALL THE WORK FOR THE DAY IS DONE OR 'TIL YOU GET PERMISSION. DO YOU UNDERSTAND ME GAL?"

Will didn't have choices about where the strap landed on my body. My pleading seemed to make him hit me harder, so I took the rest of the beating in silence. I was quiet but heard the sound of the assault on the flesh created by my daddy. I got on my knees and covered my head. At least, I thought, I can save the face my daddy made. I could tell it was the part of my flesh Will Johnson hated the most.

"ALL A Y'ALL TOO SPOILED. I GUESS 'CAUSE YOU HIGH YELLOW LIKE YO DADDY YOU THINK YOU TOO GOOD TO WORK. YOU AND CLYDE AIN'T NO BETTER THAN NOBODY ELSE AND IF I HAVE TO BEAT IT IN YOU TO MAKE YOU KNOW IT, I WILL. WHERE YO ASS BEEN? WHAT YOU DO WITH THAT ONERY ASS HORSE?"

He tried to make me tell where Malachi was, but I'd made up my mind that I'd rather take as many beatings as he could give me before I'd tell. I decided that day that I'd take everybody's beatings. After the first licks, I couldn't have hurt any worse. I thought it was never going to end but Will, out of breath, gave in before I did. He was already so out off shape he didn't even work on shoes anymore but found enough strength to try to beat my daddy out of me.

My skin was stripped, whelped, and broken. Mama pretended she didn't see it.

THIRTY-ONE

My eyes moved forward and backward on the ground. I needed to watch where I was going and keep my eyes on Clyde as our burning, bare feet moved between cotton plants and dirt. I had to make sure Clyde chopped like I told her, always moving the hoes ahead of ourselves. Will sharpened the blades of the hoes every night. It would have pleased him if one of us had cut off a toe.

Each day for us it was, chop, chop, chop as our bodies cried, thirst, thirst, thirst. Thelma's little feet didn't move fast enough to bring the water fast enough. That water bucket she had to carry was almost bigger than she was. Mama filled the buckets then stood to watch Thelma struggle to bring them to us. As she got close enough, the buckets would be almost empty from her stumbling and spilling. We drank what was left and she'd take the empty bucket back to be filled again.

Besides being thirsty most of the day, once a month, the bottom of my stomach started to cramp. When I felt the pain, Clyde let me drink most of what was left of the water, thinking my cramps were from not getting enough. It got to be so painful I thought it must have something to do with Will's daughters' cooking, so I stopped eating most of the food they cooked. Mama only watched them when she was teaching them to make a new dish. Will didn't allow complaints but one of those cramping days I begged him for relief.

"Mr. Johnson, could I please rest today. My stomach is hurting bad."

"Finish ten rows and I'll let you come in."

We never had a work limit. With left-over bread in our pockets, we always had to do as much as we could do from dawn to dusk. The misery in my stomach didn't slow me down that day. The sooner I finished, the sooner I could go to the house and rest. I had beautiful thoughts of Mama making me hot tea to soothe my stomach. She hadn't as much as laid a hand on me since she and Will got married. I wished she'd just touch my hair.

Clyde helped me finish my ten rows. She couldn't go to the house with me so I told her not to try to do the work of two while I was gone.

Pain made me press on my stomach with one hand as I threw the hoe over my shoulder with the other. I saw my shadow in front of me floating toward the house. Looking a lot longer than I thought it should, I wondered if I'd gotten a lot taller. Dry dirt between the cotton rows burned the bottoms of my feet. I stepped on Will's precious, cotton plants to try to make them feel cooler. I started to notice all the calluses and burns on my feet. Surely, I should have noticed them before but didn't. I hadn't even noticed myself getting tall. My thoughts were mostly about how our life used to be. Feeling like rest for me was near, I approached Will who was waiting on the porch.

"Where the hell do you think you're going?"

"You said if I finished ten rows, I could come in."

"I changed my mind. I don't believe you got finished that fast. Get your ass back out there before I have to knock it back out there. You better work 'til sundown. You won't get any special treatment around here."

With pain in my heart, my stomach and my hoe over my shoulder, I turned to go back but not before I saw Mama step backwards on the other side of the door, trying to keep me from seeing her.

We chopped and chopped and chopped. Day after day we were thirsty, thirsty, thirsty. Every month I cramped, cramped, cramped. On and on, same thing day after day and I didn't know the reason I hurt.

One day I didn't care what Will Johnson said. I had to leave the cotton field and was scared to death. I didn't know why, along with the cramping, blood soiled my clothes, ran down my legs and I felt faint. I staggered to the house. Emma was the one to first see me. I begged for her help.

"This is woman talk. What I'm going to say is a secret for women's ears only. You can't even talk about it to your brothers. Your body is telling you that you are no longer a child. You can't think like a child no more. You've become a woman."

"But I don't feel any different. I'm only thirteen. I can't be a woman at thirteen!"

Emma started to gather rags and folded them into a comfortable cushion, showing me how to place the cushion between my legs to catch the blood. She cut a string and tied it around my waist, pinning it to the rag bundle to hold it in place.

"Well, you're a sho nuff woman now. You can even have a baby."

"A BABY! WHAT DO YOU MEAN? I'M NOT EVEN MARRIED! MY DADDY SAID A WOMAN HAS TO BE MARRIED BEFORE SHE CAN HAVE A BABY!"

"Hush! Don't talk so loud."

"And I don't keep secrets from my brothers."

Emma scared me half to death. Blood, secrets, babies, chop, chop, cramp, cramp, thirst, thirst. I needed my mother.

I found Mama and whispered in her ear. She looked embarrassed and pushed me away.

"Didn't Emma talk to you about this?"

"Yes, but I need to talk to you. Emma said I was going to have a baby. How can I have a baby and I'm not married?"

"Emma knows what she's talking about. Whatever she tells you, believe her."

Mama acted like she couldn't wait to get away from me. All I thought about was Grandma Caroline and OH! How I needed her now.

Blood and pain came from my body at the same time every month. Each time it was leaving me, I slept well. Every time it was coming back, I worried so much about having a baby. I didn't know any better then. I grew accustomed to the exhaustion I felt from being awake all night from pain and worry and slaving all day in the midst of cotton.

One night when the blood and pain was leaving me, I was welcoming the slumber in my head and the comfort to my limbs. I thought my slumber was being interrupted by a nightmare as my ears were insulted by agonizing screams. Something was shaking my body. It was John David's gentle hand. I clearly recognized the screaming voice as Emma's.

Clyde, groggy, frightened, and confused didn't know where she was right away until I shook sense into her. I quieted John David before Clyde and I eased the door open where the noise came from. Neither of us could ever have imagined what we saw in that place we called, For Johnson Women Only. Blood was everywhere. Mary and Hattie Mae were standing on each side of Emma. Mama and a strange lady were at Emma's feet. To the surprise of Clyde and me, that night, Emma had a baby boy.

My mind raced back to Franklinton. The night Thelma and John David were born we never heard Mama even groan. I guess it was because Vee and the other women didn't allow us to be near anybody having a baby. When they let us come in the room, we never saw blood all over the place. It seems like all of us were all born in the midst of neatness.

I became more frightened. Emma already told me if I have blood coming from my body, I could have a baby too. Daddy said I had to have a husband but that night I began to believe Emma. She didn't have a husband either and she had a baby.

Everybody was so busy until I guess they didn't notice us watching. Just about the time my eyes and ears had taken as much as they could stand, Mary spotted us at the door. As we started to back away, she yelled.

"Y'all come on in here. You may as well stay and help. Get some fresh water ready so you can start washing these bloody things.'

We acted like we didn't hear and backed completely out of their sight. I squeezed Clyde's hand as she whispered in my ear.

"Sister, let's pray."

As our eyes closed to pray, we heard an angry command.

"Get back in here! Y'all heard me!"

We prayed anyway before we faced mounds of bloody towels, rags and sheets.

"Do you mean we have to touch all that bloody stuff?", I asked.

"Yes! And get moving. I want it all cleaned up before it's time for y'all to go to work."

I thought I heard Mama let out a sigh of relief.

"Come on", Mama said. "I'll show y'all what to do", as she motioned toward the pile of a bloody mess. She didn't touch one thing. Just gave us directions.

The rest of the night Clyde and I emptied bloody pails of water, refilled them with clean water. We rubbed and scrubbed blood until it was time to change from our own blood-stained gowns into our daytime cotton field wear. We had to get those seeds in the ground so Will could have himself a "good crop of cotton."

THIRTY-TWO

From the first time Will Johnson found out, he carried his shotgun everywhere but couldn't threaten anyone into telling him who got Emma pregnant. Emma wouldn't tell either. His threatening didn't scare Emma or anybody else. Her having a baby without having a husband wasn't good for his already questionable reputation or his plans to be a preacher. Emma made him grieve. Clyde and I suffered for it. We walked the floor every night trying to pacify the hungry infant Emma named, Maurice. That child cried himself into exhaustion because Emma didn't want to be awakened. She lay around moaning and groaning all day pretending she was too sick to function and slept through the child's cries at night. We fed the baby mashed up solid foods when he should have been feeding from his mother's breast. Giving him something like a warm bowl of grits and cow's milk late at night was the only way to get him pacified and us some sleep.

Spring in the field was as hard as the chopping and cotton-picking seasons. Days got longer, nights shorter and Maurice more demanding. Clyde and I could tell nobody gave him much attention when we weren't there during the day. We could hear his hollering on our way to the house like he knew it was time for us to be there. He didn't stop crying until one of us picked him up. As he grew, he acted like he wanted us to play with him all night long whether we fed him or not. Clyde and I took turns taking cat naps while Maurice was awake. We started loving him like he was our own and he loved us like he had two mothers.

Will never stopped punishing me for not telling him where Malachi was. He made us dig up the soil with sticks and hoes to sow his cotton seeds. In the spring, rain, or shine, we planted his cotton. In the scorching heat of the summer, without enough water and only bread in our pockets for a mid-day meal, we chopped the grass and weeds from around the cotton plants before those bolls cracked open waiting to be picked. In the fall, we pulled the cotton stalks out of the ground to clear the field for the next spring's planting. Will made slaves of us all for the sake of building him, the biggest sinner around, of all things, a church. Leon and David also as driven as we were, one spring, just ran away.

Will promised Mama when his daughters learned all she needed to teach them, they were going to be better women than John Ricks' daughters. The daughters mostly watched while Mama did most of the cooking and cleaning. Clyde and I slaved in the fields while Emma, Mary and Hattie Mae did little except get fatter and lazier. John Ricks' children were like slaves in Will Johnson's cotton field and Mama was a slave to Will and his daughters' every desire. Mama tried in vain to buy his approval even giving him what Daddy left for us to live on.

My brothers seldom came anymore. They hadn't been there since before Will beat me. I believe they were tired of bringing their hard, earned money to Mama while Will couldn't wait to collect it from her. Will said he needed all the money he could get to build his church.

Whenever my brothers came, they'd take some of the load off us. They'd come to the field and plow, plant, chop, pick or harvest Will Johnson's cotton. Sometimes they were there before anybody at the house knew. The field was the only place we could speak freely. I fed them information sparingly. They were big as men now. I didn't want them to get into trouble but after the beating I took, I thought a lot about whether I was going to tell them about it the next time they came. I could still feel the sting of that razor strap on my body but hadn't quite made up my mind whether to tell them how Will beat Malachi and me. They could see for themselves how Mama catered to Will and his daughters. The one thing I'd want to always convince them of was they had to remember Daddy's lessons about being obedient.

That word obedient stayed on my mind. That Bible verse, 'Honor thy father and thy mother', wouldn't leave my mind either. I had to keep believing and obeying what was taught by my daddy or I'd be dishonoring him. The Bible didn't talk about conditions. It didn't say honor Mama only if she was good. I had to heed the lessons I knew so well and make sure everybody else did too.

After my brothers left, I missed conversations we had when we were all together. Clyde and I only had each other to talk to now and her voice started to sound so tired and bewildered.

"Sister, it's a shame we don't have anybody we can trust and nobody to love us. Looks like we've been forsaken, and I don't know why. I don't trust one of those Johnson people, including Mama. Mama acts like she's a true Johnson woman now. She acts like she forgot who she is and where she came from."

I often reminded Clyde about who we were and where we came from.

"It's strange that I haven't heard from Daddy since we left Franklinton. I thought he'd come here with us. I guess this is no place for him, but I thought he'd be with us everywhere."

"Sister, what in the world are you talking about? Daddy is dead and even being dead he wouldn't be caught here!"

Clyde let out a hearty laugh, but I knew she wasn't tickled.

"Are you losing your mind, Sister? I know we need rest, but you must be more worn out than I thought. Sit down and rest. I'll work for you."

"See there! You're forgetting Daddy's lessons already. Don't you remember how Daddy said that death can't restrain a loving spirit?"

"Maybe the spirit is no longer loving. I'm surprised you still believe all that stuff. I miss daddy too but I don't believe he can come back."

"Yes, he can! But I haven't felt him around me in a long time."

With a smirk, Clyde said, "Well he needs to hurry up and come on to help us. He needs to wring Mama's neck the same way we had to wash and wring those bloody sheets and the way we have to wash and wring those messy, baby diapers from a little, bastard baby that has absolutely nothing to do with us. Ole man Johnson has made such a coward of Mama until she doesn't even want to be an important person anymore. I never thought she'd fall so low."

"What you're saying is disrespectful, Clyde. You shouldn't say bad things about her. She's our mother. I don't understand her either, but we shouldn't disrespect her. 'Honor thy father and thy mother'."

I raised my eyes from my feet when Clyde didn't answer. She pulled a small sack out of her pocket and pinched a brown powder between her thumb and forefinger, putting it in her bottom lip.

"What in the world is that?"

"It's snuff. You act like you've never seen snuff before."

"I've never seen YOU with it. When in the world did you start that?"

"That night we had to stay up washing all that bloody stuff was the first time I tried it. I'd seen those Johnson women use it so I stole some from Emma. I didn't want you to catch me using it so the first time, I swallowed it instead of spitting it out. It made me drunk. Being drunk helped that night and it helps now when we have to wash those shitty diapers. It calms my nerves too whenever I think about Mama and that ole, bastard, Will Johnson be working us from can to can't."

"Clyde, stop cursing!"

"Stop cursing? What comes out of my mouth ain't nothing like the curse that's been on us ever since Daddy died. And you have the nerve to say you haven't heard from him. Sounds like you're losing your mind. I ain't gon let these sons-a- bitches make me lose mine. I can't wait til I'm grown so I can catch the first thing leaving away from here. Our brothers left us, and we don't even hear from them much anymore. Grandma Caroline and Grandpa Frank too old now to come see bout us. Uncle Stewart is tied down with his new wife. We 'uns just out here in the world by ourselves and you got the nerve to talk about our DEAD daddy. He left us to these savages. You did get one thing right. We 'uns ain't heard from him. That ain't the worst of it. We 'uns ain't gon hear from him."

"Clyde, I'm surprised at you. You've let those Johnson people rub off on you. You don't even speak correct English anymore, saying ain't, gon, 'bout and we'uns and cursing too. I wonder what Daddy would say about that? You sound like you're the one needing rest. Daddy would never forsake us. He told us there's a time for everything. We just have to wait."

"I ain't gon wait no longer than I have to in this hell hole. You can keep waiting to hear from yo daddy. I ain't gon wait no longer than the first day I'm grown enough to find me a way out of here like our brothers did."

"You can do whatever you want but I'm not going to act like you. I'm not going to hell for being disobedient, for cursing and dishonoring Mama."

"You been obedient all this time and you're in hell just the same, right now."

Those words made me pause. They sounded like the truth.

"Let me try a pinch of that snuff."

The tobacco sting on my bottom lip made me shiver but not more than what I saw coming down the road when I raised my head.

THIRTY-THREE

Clyde saw my startled reaction, dropped her hoe, and started running. Willie, Carl and Aaron were coming down that road at last. Clyde didn't stop talking from the moment she reached them. I leaned on my hoe to wait, studying their faces as they came closer. I couldn't believe how they had grown from boys to men. I could tell by their faces what Clyde must have been saying and heard her telling them where Malachi was and how badly Will had beat me. The closer they came, the better I could hear their questions. Their deep voices sounded concerned.

"What does he mean we have to take his name? I'll be damned if I will. What in the world is wrong with Mama? She acts like she's voodooed or something."

"Hush your mouth Carl! You know there's no such thing as voodoo", I scolded. "Bite your tongue. Daddy would have a fit if he heard you say something like that."

"Take his name? We have a name that we're proud of and it's not Johnson", Aaron added.

"That's right, Aaron", Willie interrupted. That low-down dog can't make me take his name."

"We don't even get to go places where we need a name anymore", I said as I hugged them.

"That's because now he won't let us go to school", Clyde explained. "We do still go to church. Everybody there already knows our name. It doesn't matter what anybody calls me. My name is Ricks and that's all there is to it."

The sun was blazing but for some reason the heat didn't feel like it was baking us like it did before we saw my brothers. The warmth in our brothers' embraces made the temperature just right. Willie had me so wound in his arms he made my shirt rise above my waist. Carl's eyes quickly moved from Clyde's tobacco stained teeth and became fixed on my scarred back.

"Put her down, Willie."

The concerned tone in Carl's voice scared me. He lifted my big shirt to just below my breast. Willie and Aaron positioned themselves to see. As he lowered the shirt, he sounded like a general giving an order to Willie and Aaron.

"Let's go!", Carl commanded. "It's time we put Will Johnson in his place!"

Willie picked up my hoe. Aaron picked up Clyde's. Carl easily threw me over his back like I was an empty sack. Clyde ran ahead of all of us yelling,

"HOT DAMN! HOT DAMN!"

Clyde cursed. I prayed to God and Daddy.

"Lord, Lord, Lord, You and Daddy need to come on down here. I've looked for You in this cotton field. I've tried to feel You and Daddy in the fluffy bloom of this cotton and listen for the sounds of your voices in the birds' melodies. I've tried to be obedient. I've tried to honor You, my Father in heaven, my mother and to keep honoring my father who was once here on this earth. You stopped my fingers from burning, my back from hurting and helped me to sleep when I was too tired to sleep and when I thought I hurt too bad to get relief. You sustain us when we're hungry and keep us moving even when we're thirsty, so I know You and Daddy have to be somewhere near when we need both of you. I already know You and Daddy know what's best about everything so wouldn't you think You and Daddy know it's best that you all come on right now? Daddy, the boys you left are men now and there's fixing to be trouble here. We're going to need all the help we can get from you today."

My brothers' footsteps marched in synchrony. I bounced up and down off Carl's shoulder feeling light as a feather. Nobody was paying attention to my prayer, but I didn't care as long as I believed God and Daddy could hear me.

Of all the days for Carl to push the door open just in time to see Will Johnson shove Mama, this was the day! She stumbled backwards landing on the divan. Aaron raised the hoe over his head getting ready to strike Will. Carl grabbed the hoe and pushed Aaron back.

"Don't hit him Aaron. My fists will do just fine. I want to feel the licks I put on him as much as I want him to feel them."

Carl struck the first blow on Will's jaw.

"Let's see whether this woman shoveling, Sister beating, horse whipping, lazy, wannabe man has anything in him that's worth something! Pick on me, you sorry son-of-a-bitch. Pick on somebody whose name is Ricks."

Carl struck blow after blow as Will tried to cover his face and head.

Do you hear me? Ricks is our name. NOT JOHNSON!"

The popping sounds from Carl's hands on Will sounded like a whip. My brother's hands were so big I thought I should feel for sorry Will until that sound reminded me of the whip landing forcefully on Malachi's hide and that razor strap cutting my flesh.

Thelma and John David stood, frightfully, watching at the kitchen door. Maurice was in the very high-chair Daddy had made for his own babies. Clyde pushed past Aaron toward the kitchen door to get the children out of the way when she heard Aaron yell.

"Get him good, Carl but save a piece of that low-down bastard's ass for me!"

Clyde snatched Maurice out of the chair and deposited all three children on the porch. Coming back inside, she eased around the wall's edge just in time to see Will come flying by landing on and splintering the highchair.

"I knew you were coming, Daddy! You didn't make that chair for somebody's bastard baby to sit on! Kick his ass real good Carl!"

I cursed before I knew it. Clyde leaned back holding her sides she was laughing so hard. This time her laugh was real.

The whole thing was over before the Johnson sisters could wriggle their over-weight bodies out of their seats to help. Willie held them hostage with a hoe over their heads, daring them to move, anyway. Will was caught so off guard, the shock kept him from defending himself. Besides he was outnumbered. As he lay cowering on the floor, Carl picked him up and threw him out the door threatening to kill him if he ever touched any of us again, including Mama. Mama still seated, kicked her legs, and screamed.

As if it wasn't enough that he'd been beaten and thrown out of his own house, little Thelma walked up to his body, placed her little hands on her little hips and said, "Carl kick your ass, did he?"

Willie admonished, "Thelma, you're not supposed to say bad words like that!"

"Sister said it too", Thelma answered.

Willie smiled, picked his little sister up and spit toward the ground next to Will. Mama was screaming the entire time. We could still hear her screaming inside the house.

"What did y'all do to my husband? You all hurt Will! You had no right to do that!"

None of us knew what to say. We were amazed at Mama's reaction. Nobody answered her right away. Clyde was the first to speak.

"Is anybody hungry? All that moving around can make a body hungry."

Mama ran to the bedroom still whimpering and mumbling. The Johnson women were outside putting wet towels on Will's rapidly swelling face.

The table was already set but it wasn't for us. My brothers sat down while Clyde and I put that hearty meal on the table that Mama had cooked for the Johnsons. While the Johnsons sulked, the kitchen came alive with laughter and lively conversation.

Our brothers told us stories of their adventures on the railways. Carl talked about a fancy car he'd seen that he wanted to buy. Willie described a telephone which, to us, was a first. Aaron told us about cities three or maybe four times the size of Franklinton or Greensburg. We laughed, talked and sang church songs. We even exaggerated a bit. In all of that conversation, nobody mentioned what had happened earlier. We talked and ate all the food on purpose. Clyde and I enjoyed the pleasure of serving our brothers. We hadn't had the privilege of sitting at a table together since Mama married Will. The biggest surprise of all was when my brothers announced, they were going to stay a while. I didn't know how they could after what had just happened, but I did know I didn't feel tired anymore.

As I was clearing the table, Emma walked in the kitchen and snatched Maurice right out of Clyde's arms.

"Y'all's mama and we 'uns daddy want to see y'all"

Maurice was kicking and screaming and reaching for Clyde to take him back. Emma's grip was so tight on him I was afraid she was going to cut his breath off.

"Well", Carl answered standing and rubbing his stomach, "let us Rickes see just what Mr. Johnson wants."

"Wonder if he wants his behind kicked again?", Aaron asked.

Everybody laughed and went to the bedroom.

It was not surprising to see Mama looking distraught. Sitting by the window she patted tears from her face. What did surprise me was, she was holding a lace handkerchief. I hadn't seen her pull out of what was left of her beautiful things in a long while and that one seemed too beautiful to soil with tears.

The sight of Will was stunning but not surprising. His face was swollen so much it was difficult to see where his eyes separated. He had a towel in his hand and a shotgun across his lap. The sight of that gun was the biggest surprise for all of us. Carl gestured for all of us to be still. My brothers were certainly capable of defending themselves but were no match for a loaded shotgun. We didn't take our eyes off that gun while we waited for Will to speak.

"If you girls want to remain here you can keep on doing the work that you been doing and y'all can wait on your mama. For you boys, there are two roads out there. Y'all can take either one that you want that takes you away from here. I want you gone and never to come back. These are my rules."

Standing silent with their eyes barely moving from the gun, I wondered how my brothers could maybe take all of us away that night. Clyde and I fixed our eyes on Mama. She wouldn't raise her head to look at us.

"Mama?", I called.

All of us looked at her. If ever we needed her to defend us, it was now. Clyde's eyes were begging.

Mama patted her face with the corner of her handkerchief as she raised her head. Before she spoke, she looked back and forth at each of us, directly in our eyes. She looked away from us toward Will then back at us with the expression of a decaying turnip.

"Children! This is my husband!"

My body felt icy cold. In the chill, my eyes danced back and forth from Mama to Will to the shotgun. Could this be the answer to my prayer? Surely, not! I didn't feel that I could ever pray another prayer. For the first time in my life I didn't believe there was really a God or any such thing as a spirit, especially a loving spirit. Again, I felt so tired.

THIRTY-FOUR

For a fire to burn, it must be poked and stirred. Kindling must be piled on and around it to keep the flames sparkling. I couldn't feel any fire within me for fear of it going out. I didn't want to be poked or stroked and I knew Uncle Stewart didn't understand it when I resisted his trying to hug me. With no warmth inside me, I felt like I was freezing all over.

I listened to Uncle Stewart giving Mama the news and watched her doubtful expression like she didn't believe he was telling her the truth. She rocked so forcefully, I thought the chair was going to fall off the edge of the porch. Uncle Stewart was still and looked serious as he spoke. She must have thought Uncle Stewart was going to give Will a beating too. She saw him coming before he got to the door, rushed out and offered him a seat on the porch.

Will didn't come out to greet Uncle Stewart or to order me and Clyde back to the field. He stood just inside the open door like he was hiding but close enough to eavesdrop.

"How did you get the news about Daddy before me? Mama would have written to me before she told you he was sick."

"Marjanna, I don't know how I can prove to you what your mother said. I'd never tell a lie on our mother", Uncle Stewart said with a tremble in his voice.

Will heard the anger in Uncle Stewart's voice. He cracked the door open. He kept a safe, cowardly distance and with just his head sticking out he interrupted the conversation.

"Marjanna, let one of the girls go to help your mama. We can spare one of them. We're just about finished with this year's crop anyway. Let Clyde go."

Uncle Stewart stood up and walked toward the door.

"SISTER will go! That's who Mama asked for."

Will quickly shut the door saying, "I ain't getting into no family mess. Suit yourself."

"And I'm going to take Thelma and John David with me!", I added.

I felt confident to say anything now with Uncle Stewart there. Will wasn't going to protest. He was too afraid. Mama wasn't either after I said I was going to take Thelma and John David with me. Clyde wasn't going to be able to do everything by herself and she would have to do more if the little ones stayed.

I didn't have to do much to get ready to go. All I had were pieces of things adding up to nothing-tattered clothes, no shoes, a precious piece of hair wrapped in a piece of cloth tied with a faded, blue ribbon, a wooden heart with the initials S.B. and C.R. carved in the middle, a letter written by my Uncle David on a faded piece of paper and a precious heart of gold.

I watched Clyde watching me. She stayed right on my heels, sometimes whispering.

"Sister, I hate for you to leave me here with this trash. They're like rabid dogs. With you gone it's no telling what's going to happen to me now."

"I don't want you to worry Clyde. I'll bet our brothers told Grandma what's happening to us. Grandma is trying to prevent bloodshed and I'll bet she hasn't told Grandpa everything our brothers told her. Will knows now that he's treading on dangerous ground. He's nothing but a coward anyway and probably won't do anything like he did before. I'll also bet that Grandma has a plan. I know how she thinks. Our brothers are somewhere helping Grandma make a way for all of us to get away from here without anybody getting hurt or in trouble. Grandma has always said, where there are angry men there's trouble and where there's trouble there's death. Be patient Clyde. Nothing's going to happen to you now.

THIRTY-FIVE

Grandma walked down the road to meet the wagon because she said Uncle Stewart was moving too slow. She kept repeating, "Lord! Lord! Lord!" as she looked me over.

Grandma rubbed lard on my hands and feet until the calluses vanished. She bathed my back, soothing it with pure lanolin making the scars fade. I hadn't felt a brush on my hair since we moved in with those Johnsons. Our nicest things went missing in their house. I would fall asleep while Grandma brushed life back into my broken strands. I hadn't had shoes on in so long I thought Grandma had given me a size too small. The soft, knitted slippers she made would do until I could get used to having real shoes again. She cooked all the time making us eat something whether we were hungry or not. She didn't allow me to do much for Thelma and John David. She took care of them too. Said I'd done enough work to last the rest of my life.

Grandma was pouring all the love she had inside of herself onto me. Although calluses vanished from my hands and feet and scars no longer claimed spaces on my back and she stirred love in the food she fixed that nourished and rounded my body to its fullest, I'd never looked better on the outside but I couldn't feel anything on the inside. Even when Grandma talked, I couldn't feel how to respond.

"Sister, your mama is different from my other children. She was born with a weak mind. Even you can see that. She can't help it. Your grandfather has a weak mind. For years he gambled away almost everything we had, and I didn't say a word. That shows how weak I am too. When there's a flaw in the blood some folks think there's nothing you can do about it but there is. I'm a living witness to that. I should have stood up to your grandfather long before I did. When I did stand firm, it made a difference. Your mama inherited one side of her weakness from your Grandpa Frank and one side from me. One day she'll find strength from somewhere to overcome her weakness like your grandfather and I did."

Grandma could tell I couldn't think of anything to say.

"Your mama had never been as stable as she was until after she married your father. Your father loved her a lot and she loved him too. She hates him now because he died. That's just the way she thinks. She can't help herself."

Well, by then, I'd heard just about enough without speaking. Now, I knew just what I wanted to say.

"Daddy showed me how animals protect their babies from harm. Mama doesn't protect any of us. She knows Mr. Johnson can't stand me and when he mistreats me she doesn't say one word to defend me. She mistreats me too just to please him. She loves having a man more than she cares about her own children and any man will do. She allowed him to take almost everything from her just to keep him around. I hate Mr. Johnson, his daughters and......"

Grandma interrupted, "Please don't say you hate your mama. I don't want you to have to pay for something you'll probably regret later, Sister. Your body is healing but your heart isn't. Don't let your heart harden more than it already is. I want to see you as that soft, sweet girl you were when your father was alive. Open your heart and let that cold blood run out and the warmth flow in. The world you knew when your father was alive is still out there. Nothing has changed but you."

"Grandma, speaking about the body and blood, will you tell me how I can have a baby and I'm not married?"

Grandma's changing the subject to tell me how my body works was the only thing that made me feel better. When she finished telling me what had to happen to get a baby, I didn't think I'd ever be pregnant.

THIRTY-SIX

No matter what Grandma said, most of my sadness stayed with me. She didn't stop trying to help. She asked Monroe to come take me for a ride. I didn't want to go without knowing where he was going to take me. I also thought since most of my world was different now, I believed everything I used to know had to be different too.

The sun was barely visible that morning when Monroe drove up. He and his horse were fresh as a new day rising. I could see dew sparkling from green patches of clover and smelled the sweet fragrance of honeysuckle as we rode quietly along. The fragrances had never been almost hypnotizing until that day. Moving along that familiar road that was well endowed with the same sturdy, patriarchal and matriarchal oaks that were still staking claims in their long ago, well established places brought back memories of conversations that arose quietly in my mind. Music charmed my senses as the church steeple came into view. The imaginary smell of smoking meat choked words from my mouth making me tell Monroe everything that happened since we left Franklinton. Monroe was quiet. I wouldn't have known he was listening except every now and then as his head nodded, he'd reach over to squeeze my hand. When the wagon stopped in front of Crystal Springs African Methodist Episcopal Church, he handed me a wrapped bundle he took from the back of the wagon.

Childhood memories flooded and crowded every space in my head. The sound of the organ made me rush inside. I suddenly remembered how much I had loved Sunday services at Crystal Springs Church. Until I walked into the cemetery, I'd forgotten how to love the sight of colorful flowers. My mind had come to see only white cotton. I hadn't given living, loving spirits many thoughts until my knees rested in front of my brothers' and Daddy's graves. I dug in the ground, placing flowers from Monroe's bundle. While the soil was coming alive, I felt my spirit being lifted up. It was then and there that I knew I could make a way out of no way. Mine had been a long, lost soul suddenly being found. I even thought I could hear Daddy's voice reading to Monroe, "Don't build a shell around your loving heart that's so hard you can't emit the love that's within you."

Like stone pillars, heavy weights of despair fell off me until I felt light enough to know my good spirit was rising on up. I knew now, I could face anything, even Mama and those Johnsons. I could even toil in Will Johnson's cotton fields and not faint. I could endure punishment for my brothers and sisters even if it meant my own body being bruised. Daddy's children would always be better than Will Johnson's children. I wanted to be obedient and honor my mother the rest of my days. I was sure, for the second time in my life, there was new birth. I was being born again.

THIRTY-SEVEN

Uncle Stewart and Grandma weren't telling the truth about Grandpa Frank being sick. Except that he didn't see too well anymore, Grandpa's body wasn't sick, but his way of life was. Grandma Caroline threatened to shoot his gambler friends if they came near their house after she caught him trying to pay a gambling debt with one of their cows. She fired the shot gun leaving the men scrambling, trying not to be hit. Grandma said she never felt so good because those men haven't been back. I believe, like I, she was born again too. She just didn't know it like I did. Everybody kept an eye on Grandpa. Even before Aunt Martha and Aunt Ida moved to New Orleans they helped Grandma spy on him.

Grandma handled all the money and important matters. To make sure all their assets were in safe places, she kept only just enough of what she and Grandpa needed. She gave the horses to Uncle Stewart and Uncle Oliver. She split most of their cash with Aunt Ida and Aunt Martha. If Grandpa wanted to gamble, he had to walk to find the place and beg somebody for money to get in the game. Word spread about Grandma firing the gun so none of those men hung around him anymore. Every now and then he'd find a way to get there with the help of some unsuspecting soul.

If he left home, he had to be brought back very close to the house because he couldn't see well enough to find his own way.

Grandpa sat on the porch a lot, dreaming about getting away. His eyes worked overtime trying to discern whoever was approaching, knowing he didn't have any friends left to come take him to commit his usual sin. One day his ears perked up toward the sound of wagon wheels approaching and what he thought was a familiar bray. He waited for the sound of Grandma's footsteps and the sound of a cocking gun. He wasn't able to know it was Uncle Stewart's wagon until he heard Clyde's voice yelling, "Grandpa! Grandpa!'

I started screaming Malachi's name. I declare, I think Grandpa completely forgot how miserable he was. He was happy knowing Uncle Stewart was bringing Mama, Clyde and Malachi.

"Well! Well! Well! Ain't it 'bout time", Grandpa asked Clyde as he held her face close to his to see it better. He kissed her forehead.

Mama pushed Clyde to the side and gave Grandpa the biggest hug I'd seen her give anybody in a long time.

"Daddy I'm surprised at how well you seem to be. I was worried that you were a lot sicker than you look."

Thelma and John David hid inside when they saw it was Mama coming. I coaxed them outside to give Malachi water. They eventually talked to him and even got on to take a ride.

Uncle Stewart would have been on his way back home sooner if Malachi hadn't acted like he wanted to hang around for a while. Getting that horse to leave wasn't easy. It was like I thought I was going to need Willie there to help. Uncle Stewart said if he lived to be a hundred, he didn't think he'd ever see another horse as crazy as ours.

Riding slowly away he winked his eye at me and Grandma, motioning his head toward Clyde. Mama pretended she came to see about us and

Grandpa. Uncle Stewart was letting us know that Clyde had a lot to tell. Mama was trying to leave Will Johnson.

Clyde told us how Mr. Johnson started being away from home more than he was there. He didn't allow Mama to question his whereabouts. This time Mama wanted to leave while Will was away. When he came home and found her gone, she thought, he'd miss her and come looking for her. Clyde told us how she talked about Will all the way from Greensburg to Washington Parish and didn't stop even after she got there. She didn't say one word about the scars no longer visible on me or the glow in our skin or the healthy whiteness in our eyes or the roundness in our well-fed bodies. Will Johnson was the only subject she'd speak about.

"He'll go looking for me at Stewart's house first. After he finds out I'm not there, he'll know for sure I'm here. I wish he'd hurry up and come get me. I want to go home. I thought about leaving him for good and would do it today if I could find me another man today. He doesn't do anything for me and my children, but I love him anyway. Every woman needs herself a man."

We were astonished by her words and her talking was constant.

"If I let Will go, somebody else will just snatch him up. I can't let folks think I can't hold on to my man. Those busy bodies at church are always staring at me funny. It's none of their business anyway. I don't care what they think or say. I'm going to hang on to my man."

After weeks passed without a sign of Will Johnson, Mama stopped talking so much. Grandma started getting up during the night finding her sitting on the porch gazing down that empty road leading to the house. I felt sorry for her. Her body was frail. Dark circles came back around her eyes. She looked a lot like she did when Daddy died. The rest of us were happy until she started all that crying again. I lost hope of her being born again like me and Grandma. I started wishing for Uncle Stewart to come back and take her back to where she thought was her home. I wished her to be happy like the rest of us even if it meant she was with Will.

Grandma and Grandpa didn't want Mama to go back to Will's house at first but watching her brood and seeing her wasting away again drove them to their wits' end. Grandma sent for Uncle Stewart and Mama started packing all of our things. Grandma begged her to let us stay.

"When I go, everybody's going with me. Will probably is missing all of us."

John David didn't want to leave Grandma's side. Thelma screamed, "I'm not going! I'm not going!"

Grandma worried so much until her head ached so bad, she'd tie a scarf around it so tight it put creases in her forehead. Watching my grandmother in pain was almost more than I could take.

"Grandma, it's alright. We'll be fine. I can take care of everybody and I'm strong enough now to endure anything that happens."

"Sister, with all of you going back there, I'll never rest well, again."

"Grandma I know you trust God. I know you know that God is in me the same as was in my daddy. If you're trusting God, then you must also know that's the same kind of trust you must have that's inside of me. I'm stronger now. I'll know what to do if anything happens. I can't let Mama go back there by herself. Right or wrong, she's my mother."

"Sister, you sound just like you've grown into a woman, right before my eyes. That softness is back in you. I'm proud that you're my grandchild. I really mean my GRANDWOMAN!"

THIRTY-EIGHT

Maurice twisted and wriggled his little body until Emma had to let him go. She couldn't keep him inside the door when he saw us coming. If she'd held him any tighter, she could have broken his arm. She watched, halfway in and halfway out of the door as she peeped.

"How's your father?"

The question from Emma stunned Mama. Except for the day she got to Washington Parish, she hadn't been concerned with how Grandpa was. She never even asked Grandma any questions about his dimming eyesight. She ignored Emma's question.

"What did Will say about me being away? Did he miss me? Did he want to come and get me?"

"He hasn't mentioned you one time."

"Is he going to leave me?" What's on his mind, Emma?"

"I don't know what's on his mind."

Emma never looked directly at Mama as she gave those short answers.

I began to notice how she or her sisters never went outside. They wanted me to keep the doors closed. They avoided having much contact with us acting like they were afraid we might ask the wrong question. I just knew, something bad was going to happen. I could feel it. I started planning how to protect Clyde, Thelma, John David and even Mama from something I could feel was dreadfully inevitable. All that good rest I got at Grandma's house was preparing me for all that was going to happen.

From the time I got back to Will's house I didn't get much sleep. I walked the floor at night watching over everyone else while they slept. I wore my clothes under my night gown and put the little ones to sleep half dressed. Clyde wasn't curious enough to notice the difference. I didn't tell her what I was doing. I didn't want her to worry or her to start acting suspicious. Something just told me to stash a change of clothes for all of us including Mama. I cooked more food than was necessary, packing and storing leftovers in places where I could easily grab them in a rush. My fine-tuned ears filtered ordinary night sounds, focusing on what was unusual. Trying not to make a mistake about what I could hear, I didn't understand how Will sneaked up on me, one night, while I was pumping water. He scared the daylights out of me when he touched my shoulder.

"Oh! Mr. Johnson! What's the matter with you, tipping up on me like that? I almost dropped this water."

"Be quiet and hurry up and get in the house. Open the back door for me."

From the back door, I could see tiny, flickering lights in the distance. Will leaned so hard against the door that he fell forward to the inside. He struck the table where I had sat the water pitcher, knocking it to the floor.

The sound of breaking glass didn't disturb the Johnson sisters due to their over-indulgence of whiskey every night, but the noise brought Mama running. When she laid her eyes on Will, she burst into happy tears. I left that repulsive sight to awaken Clyde.

I shook Clyde gently to awaken her with one hand and covered her mouth with the other to keep her quiet.

"Get up Clyde", I whispered.

"What's the matter?", she whispered back.

I put her clothes in her hands.

"Something's going to happen. I can feel it. Get your clothes on then help me with the little ones. We're leaving and we're taking Maurice with us too."

Without question, Clyde obeyed. I was pleased she trusted what I said.

We heard Mama pleading with Will to tell her where he'd been. She was begging him not to leave without her again.

"Marjanna, these peckerwoods are coming after me, again. They're bragging about getting me for real this time. I believe that ole, evil wife of mine must have told them where to find me. They been trying to force me to work on the road. They think I still got money and hate me for it. I ain't got nothing like I used to have. How much you got? I need money to keep on running."

"Running? Run where?"

"I don't know where. All I know is I gotta get away from here tonight before something bad happens. I'll really be in trouble if I have to kill one of them. I been dodging them for weeks leading them wrong. I ain't gonna be no white man's slave. Give me the money. If I can just make it to the train, I can get a long way away from here."

"What about the children?"

"Whose children? You the only one with children. Mine are all grown. They already know this house is theirs' if I have to leave. I ain't letting no children slow me down even if I have to leave you too."

"You can't leave me. I still have a little bit of money. Do you care about anybody but yourself, Will?"

I didn't hear Will's answer. My thoughts stayed on Will talking about not being anybody's slave. He could pretend to own slaves, the way he treated us, but he couldn't be one.

Mama was surprised when she walked in the room to see us dressed and looking like we were ready to go.

"How did you all know what to do?"

"Sister always knows what to do and when to do it."

I was surprised at Clyde's answer. I wondered if she was feeling something too.

"Mama, we can leave here without Will."

Mama acted like she didn't hear me.

"Sister, all of us can't travel together safely. You and Thelma take the path southwest. Don't go in a straight line. When you get near the train tracks stay out of sight until you hear the train coming. Wait 'til it stops before you start to run to it. We'll go in a different direction and catch the train at a different stop. Act like you don't know us when you see us get on."

I thought about catching a train going in the opposite direction to get away from Will and Mama but remembered my promise to honor Mama and be obedient. She reached for John David. I pulled him back.

"Mama, I'm taking John David with me."

"No, you're not! Clyde's going with me. She can take care of John David. Thelma is enough for you to handle."

Shame! Shame! I felt for Mama. She didn't trust herself being with Will by herself. She'd stoop so low as to depend on a ten-year-old girl to protect her.

"I heard the things Will said about us. He doesn't care about us, but we care about each other. You can go with Will if you want but the rest of us are going to stay together. Maurice too. The only reason I'm going with you at all is because you're my mother and I have to be obedient. I reached inside the safe for the sacks of food I had stashed. From under the table I snatched the bag full of our clothes that we wouldn't have had if it weren't for our grandparents. I was moving so fast I didn't realize my feet were still bare until I felt them stinging. I hadn't had the time to consider broken glass scattered on the floor. Blood tracks followed me. Mama pulled dish rags from the shelf, slowing me long enough to wrap my bleeding foot before she pushed me out the door. Clyde was already waiting at the edge of the woods on the opposite side of flickering lights in the distance with John David, Thelma and Maurice. I stood still for a moment. I did it on purpose. It felt good for Mama to touch me.

We ran a while, walked fast a while, and rested little. By the time John David was wide awake, he started screaming. We stopped long enough to get him pacified. Trekking along, we started letting the little ones run along with us. My arms were numb from carrying John David and the sack of food. I knew Clyde must have felt numbness too from carrying Maurice and the clothes. We told the boys they were strong as Willie, Carl, and Aaron. Telling them that made them run as hard as they could when we put them down. Thelma didn't have much of a problem keeping up. As I was leaving a trail of blood, I thought, so what! It wouldn't be the first time.

At last, I saw a clearing and shining steel ahead. At least we'd made it to the railroad tracks but weren't yet out of danger. I told everybody to sit on the ground while we stuffed food in our mouths. We'd hardly caught our breath when we heard the train whistle. Clyde and I put on scarves pulling them toward the front to just about cover our eyes. We started running from the woods when we saw the train slowing, jumping on as soon as it stopped. There were enough empty seats for us not to have to sit close to anyone. With our heads bowed, neither Clyde nor I allowed our eyes to meet another's. The little ones went to sleep almost before we could take our seats.

Each time the train slowed my heart was like it was going to jump in my mouth. All I thought about was whether Mama was going to make it. I hoped she did, but I wished Will didn't make it. My hopes were short-lived. Will came on at the next stop. My goodness! My goodness! Where was Mama?

At first Will walked right past us, came back and took a seat right across from us. When I felt the urge to turn around to look, I saw Mama sitting behind us. She had to have already been back there when we got on. We were too relieved and too busy getting seated to notice. Will eventually moved to a seat behind her.

I dozed for what seemed like a just a minute, awakened by screeching, jerking and slowing of the train. I could tell something was wrong when another passenger asked, "What are you stopping here for?" I was thinking we couldn't be at another scheduled stop this fast.

Looking out the window I couldn't miss that herd of horses mounted by angry, white men. Several were already standing and jumped through the doors as soon as they opened.

"Everybody take a section. I'll take the back", one man yelled.

The voice was so familiar that it scared me. I was tempted to look up but knew I shouldn't.

"Look in everybody's face and look for a bloody foot", another man voice echoed down the aisle.

One man to each section awakened sleeping passengers to look at their feet and in their faces. I kept my head down and my bloody foot tucked under me. I could see glancing from the corners of my eyes that Clyde didn't bow her head. She watched, not taking her eyes off the man searching in our section. The man was joined by another stopping right by our seat. Clyde still didn't bow her head. One of them tapped lightly on my folded leg with his stick.

"Hold your head up, gal so I can see your face!"

Just as I started to lift my head a third man walked down the aisle, the three of them blocking the view from the other searchers. I pulled my scarf further to the front and slowly lifted my head. Standing in front of me, staring, were the most beautiful, crystal, blue eyes I'd recognize anywhere.

"Let me see both feet", he yelled.

I eased my foot from under me, but I couldn't stop staring. He flinched when he saw the blood-soaked, dish rag bandage. His beautiful, blue eyes filled with tears. He reached under his shirt, pulled out a package that he dropped in my lap before he dismissed the others.

"They're not on this train!", he yelled. Let's go!"

I was positive no one was ever going to know we were on that train. No one was ever going to know about tightly wrapped, clean bandages and iodine dropped in my lap.

Out the window I saw angry, disappointed, male faces mounting tired horses, all but three. Standing stoically by their horses, the trio of tall men watched the train roll by. I wanted to scream out to beg to look into Steven's eyes one more time. Monroe and Vee must have been proud of their grown-up sons. All three, so brave and handsome had grown so tall. I'd grown up knowing how to read their sad faces that also told me, Godspeed.

THIRTY-NINE

I looked backwards until Steven Blackburn was no longer in my sight. Then, I stayed turned around until I couldn't see Louisiana. I was leaving colorful magnolia trees dominating the landscape. Black-eyed Susan, wisteria and wild azaleas lay snugly among maple and sycamore. Spanish moss cuddled up to live oak, clutching so as not to ever be free. The moss held on like I'd been trying to hold on to Steven's eyes. I tried to grasp tightly to Grandma and Grandpa, Crystal Springs Church, my daddy's, and brother's graves, Starcie, William, Walter, Uncle Stewart and always back to Steven's eyes. Let it go! Let it go! a voice told me. Let it pass for now but store all of it in your heart.

I didn't let it go but yet, began to soak up scenes of Mississippi. We passed places with funny names like McComb and Grenovle, places I'd never heard my brothers speak of. I made up my mind to turn to ask Mama the way to pronounce Grenovle just as the train was pulling into a town called Mound Bayou. By this time all of us were calm.

Clyde and I didn't wait for Mama and Will. We jumped off to explore this town. The post office inside the general store was the place we could write Grandma Caroline a note. What was surprising was to see the man that waited on us wasn't a white man. He looked like us. Colored men and women strolled with a spirit in their stride that made us feel proud. They patted John David and Maurice on their heads, picked Thelma up and kissed her cheeks and complimented Clyde and me. I couldn't figure out what kind of place this was. Seeing all these things that were different made Clyde start talking before we even got closer to Mama.

"We never saw colored people in charge of places like the General Store and the Post Office. Where are the white people?"

Clyde's words came out so fast, Mama's hand gesture meant HALT! I wanted an answer quickly, too.

"What kind of place is this?"

Mama turned toward me pressing her forefinger on her lips.

"Stop acting like you're from the country."

We answered in unison.

"WE ARE FROM THE COUNTRY!"

"I never heard of a place where there aren't any white people."

"Sister don't talk so loud. Let's ask Will."

"I want to stay here."

I thought, Clyde must really like Mound Bayou. I wished we could stay too.

"Go ahead and ask Will", Clyde said.

I wondered what it must be like to live in an all colored town but not bad enough to ask Will.

"We can't stay here. Will wants us to go farther north to Marigold. He wants to be closer to Memphis."

Why Memphis? What's wrong with here?", Clyde protested.

"We just can't stay", Mama emphasized.

"We can stay anywhere we want. What you mean is Will can't stay here. We're not running from anyone. Will is."

"Don't you get impudent with me, young lady! Get back on the train."

There were hardly any slickers like Will in Marigold. I even wondered why he didn't want to live in Mound Bayou where it seems he could have hidden out easier. It was a place where all the men looked like him. He went in and out of Memphis freely. I even wondered why he didn't go there to live. It was a place larger in size and had more places to hide. I'd never thought of Will being smart enough to reason like that especially after having a man around like my daddy.

FORTY

Mama wasn't pleased about having to live in Marigold but anywhere was better than her having to live without Will Johnson. For the first time in her life since she left home, she lived on property that wasn't owned by her husband. For the first time in her life she had to pay rent. Will wasn't there most of the time and claimed not to have any money when he did come. She started taking in other people's laundry, starching and ironing their frilly, lace curtains, washing their fine linens and beautiful clothes in order to make ends meet. She resented having to touch other people's lovely things that weren't half as good as those she used to own.

Mama wrote Grandma begging for money. If she could have had her way she would have made Clyde and me stay home to help her with the laundry but Grandma said she would only send money if Clyde and I went to school and as long as we didn't have to work. Mama didn't want stipulations but didn't have a choice. Grandma sent Mama's envelope separate from the one she sent for Clyde and me. She didn't want Will to get his hands on our money and she sent enough for us not to have to ask Mama for anything.

Carl rode the train to Marigold bringing clothes Grandma made for Thelma, John David and Maurice. Besides the money Grandma sent, Carl brought money from Willie, Aaron and himself so Clyde and I would always have enough to buy our own. One day when Carl came, he brought a letter to Mama from Rozella Robinson.

Our teacher in Marigold knew Rozella Robinson. We found out the teacher had once lived in Washington Parish. She and Rozella had been writing each other ever since she found out where we came from and every since Rozella found out we were there. The teacher wanted to know what kind of student I had been in Franklinton. Surprisingly, Rozella was complimentary. The teacher told Mama how she thought I would thrive in a city school and needed more knowledge than what was offered in this tiny, country town. She recommended Mama let me go to school in Memphis. Mama explained, she didn't know anyone in Memphis. The teacher knew somebody. She knew Rozella's sister, Roxie, who lived in Memphis.

Grandma Caroline sent a letter demanding that Mama let me go. Mama, also surprisingly, didn't need too much persuasion. As a matter of fact, it brought the true Marjanna Ricks Johnson back to life. If Mama didn't get a thrill out of boasting about her children, pig aint pork. She bragged all over Marigold. She told people about her sons working on the railroad, her beautiful daughters Thelma and Clyde, her handsome son John David and her brilliant daughter Claudie who was so smart she was going to Memphis to go to school. When they'd ask about Maurice Mama just answered, "He's ours too."

I wasn't sure about going to Memphis and nobody asked me. It was feeling bitter sweetness. Thoughts of going to school in Memphis were exciting but on the other hand I had doubts about leaving my brothers and sisters alone with Mama. I was especially concerned about John David because Daddy didn't give him a partner so I assigned myself to be his partner. I asked Daddy for his forgiveness. I knew he'd understand because

I'd taken care of John David and Maurice like they were my own as much as I could. Clyde helped and took care of Thelma the same way.

Clyde and I taught the children lessons and told them about the Rickes of South Carolina. We told them about Daddy and taught them his lessons everyday. I was satisfied that their learning was well on its way and I knew I had to do what Grandma wanted or she wouldn't send money. I decided I had to go so I wouldn't be responsible for the family's deprivation. Will Johnson had caused us enough pain so I made up my mind faster.

After all was settled, I wrote Roxie Robinson asking her to tell me all about Memphis and LaRose School where I'd be attending. I felt her warmth oozing from the ink that composed the words on the paper when she answered. Miss Roxie let me know she'd be happy to have me come live with her. She painted a beautiful picture of a beautiful school in a beautiful and exciting city.

FORTY-ONE

John David liked for us to tell him what a big boy he was, and he tried really hard to act like one. Six years is too old for a boy to throw a tantrum, but John David threw one that rivaled any toddler at the train station the first day I was leaving for Memphis. He screamed so loud, kicked, and tugged so hard on my dress, disturbing all the people so much that Mama had to leave with him before the train pulled off. I was haunted all the way to Memphis by his pleading cry. I rubbed my hands together imagining I could still feel his curly, black hair that I'd always rub if he needed to be consoled. If I closed my eyes, I saw his light, brown eyes. I wanted to walk with him to school on his first day. I wanted to be the one to tell him how smart he was and watch his happiness when he learned something new. I wanted to be the first to listen when he learned to read a Bible verse. I couldn't do any of that now. I had to depend on Clyde, and she was only eleven. The only comfort I found was in knowing I'd be coming home every Friday and if I were needed, Marigold was just a short train ride away.

As exciting as Memphis and LaRose school was, neither was as pleasing as catching the train back to Marigold on Fridays. Clyde, Thelma, Maurice and John David were always there to meet me. Leaving Marigold for Memphis on Sundays was the opposite of my coming back. John David never failed to scream and to have his grip forced from my clothes. I started to feel really bad every time I left. Studying became hard. The more I tried, the more my mind drifted. Leaving Marigold dominated my thoughts with the fear of something I didn't know.

One Friday, no one came to meet me. It wasn't like Clyde to be late for anything. My mind raced with questions. Had Will caused them to have to run away again? If so, how was I ever going to find them? Where was I going to spend the night? This time I'd bought gifts for everybody and didn't even have enough for train fare back to Memphis. I would have had to wait until the post office opened again to see if a letter had arrived from Grandma.

I searched with my eyes and saw a fine car like one I'd never seen in Marigold. I admired the pretty car, but it didn't stop my worried head or calm my anxious heart. Suddenly, big hands squeezed my shoulders tightly from behind, enough to keep me from jumping out of my skin. At the same time the bass voice whispered, "BOO!"

My mind raced. Big hands? Deep voice? I knew who it was before he whirled me around.

"Carl! What a pleasant surprise! How long have you been in Marigold? I'm so glad to see you. Are Willie and Aaron here too?"

"Can you be quiet long enough for me to talk. I can answer only one question at a time. Come on. We'll talk while we ride."

I couldn't help but scream when it was obvious that we were headed toward that beautiful, black Model T that I admired.

Carl was quiet as not to spoil my admiration of his car. I wasn't fooled, though. His face and voice were somber.

"Sister, John David is sick. Clyde is doing the best she can without any help. Mama has been gone to Jackson with Will for quite a while."

"Forget about Mama and Will! What's wrong with John David? Has a doctor seen him?"

"We have to take him all the way to Mound Bayou to see a doctor. We got here last night but wanted to wait for you."

"Why all the way to Mound Bayou? I saw a doctor here in Marigold."

"But you know he's white. He won't go to colored peoples' houses and won't let colored people come to him."

"It wasn't like that in Franklinton. What kind of doctor is that? You said we. Willie and Aaron are here too, aren't they?

"You won't let me surprise you."

"You surprised me with this car. Can you drive faster. I want to get to John David."

Carl's head shook in disgust as he pulled in front of Will's and Mama's leanto.

"Did you ever think Mama would be living in something like this?"

There had been times when I thought Mama would never live in a shack but now that so much had changed, I knew that she would. It was happening now. I didn't answer Carl. Right then, it didn't matter. I wanted to get inside to see about my little brother,

John David's body was hot and dry. He was burning with fever. He tried to keep his pale, pleading eyes open as his weakened hand reached for my face.

"We have to get to Mound Bayou now! Let's go!"

Sometimes grimness can't be hidden in doctors' faces when they speak about the gravely ill. I'd seen it before when Daddy was sick. I heard him say the word diphtheria and not much more. It made no difference to me how John David caught it. That's what the doctor was trying to explain to us. All I knew was I had to get John David well or die myself trying. I bundled my little brother in quilts, nestled him, rocked, and prayed.

I asked God for more strength than I thought I already had for me to be able to endure another hurt. I needed more courage now to accept what I already knew was about to happen. I understood everything now. Another pre-destined event was about to unfold.

Daddy had done something none of us understood at the time when he didn't assign John David a partner. I'd tried to be his partner. It didn't work. Being sent to Memphis helped it not to work and every Sunday John David pleaded for me not to go. I know now that my being here wasn't going to change anything except John David wouldn't have had to beg me to stay. A storm I'd tried to ignore had been raging on my insides. The storm wasn't of good or evil. It was just destiny. Knowing was never going to leave me again. What the heart is relaying to the head should never be ignored.

I was still sitting, still rocking, still holding John David's dead body when Will and Mama came. Mama screamed the same words over and over.

"I knew he was coming back to get him! I knew he was coming back......."

All I wanted then was to carry John David to Crystal Springs Cemetery where he'd be with Percy, Otsey and Daddy. Will said no. Mama obeyed Will even at a time like that. Mama buried our brother in alien ground. Grandma Caroline came. I don't think she ever got over John David's funeral not being in church but at the cemetery. Will stood over the grave reciting incomprehensible Bible verses. Most of his words from the Bible were wrong.

Grandma was too weak to fight when I begged her not to make me go back to Memphis to school. I tried to convince her that I needed to stay to take care of Thelma and Maurice so Clyde could stay in school since Mama had started to follow Will everywhere. John David wasn't cold before Will told Mama we were going to move again. I stayed and started getting things together. It was so soon that Mama hadn't unpacked her things from the last time.

We lived in every little town and hollow south of Memphis. We had to run in the middle of the night with Will dragging Mama all over the place the same way it seemed he was dragging her the day I discovered them walking down the road to our house in Greenburg. The only difference in then and before was, he didn't have a horse to lead. This time it was only Mama.

With one eye and both ears wide open, I listened for the sound of barking dogs and watched for flickering lights in the darkness. I preached to Clyde how we must never be submissive women like our mother and made her promise, with her hand on Daddy's Bible, not to be. We wouldn't let Thelma be made to grow up to be like a woman before she finished being a little girl the way it had been for us. I made Clyde promise to protect everybody including Mama if something happened to me. She promised to remind the little ones often, of just how proud those Ricks men were. I wanted her to call their names, David Ricks Sr., David Ricks Jr. and our daddy, John Ricks when she spoke about them. We talked about Aunt Adeline's four-leaf clovers and Aunt Daphne's gold locket, her black braid and their special meanings. Clyde was to always acknowledge her namesake, Grandma Clyde Ricks and the like sweetness that was inside of her.

I told her how we were compelled to hold on to all the strengths and secrets that had been passed to us and how we must be wary of and not yield to the weaknesses that came from the Cryer side. Grandpa's weakness would have allowed him to gamble away all his possessions if Grandma hadn't overcome her submissiveness. Mama was twice as damaged as either but that's what was in her and she didn't fight it. We would fight it. We had to recognize the storms of life as they were forecast, accept them, and never ignore what is inherent within us. We had to strive to know the difference. All these things had grown in me. It was time now for Clyde to grow and know.

It was time for Clyde to understand the feeling she got when we were told we were moving on to Jonestown, Mississippi. Our discernment was the same. We already could tell by our insides that this was one of the worst placed to live. In 1923, the year we moved there, they were still hanging people just for the sport of it. Colored men and women were ordered to drop their heads and step off the sidewalk when whites were passing. Why in the world would Will Johnson, the man who was running from white men, want to live in a place like that?

FORTY-TWO

Keeping watch, not knowing when we'd have to run again made me exhausted and sometimes the exhaustion made me sleep soundly. One night I was awakened by howling winds sounding so boisterous the walls trembled. I was afraid that old, tin roof was going to cave in and cut us into pieces. Through all of that storm noise I heard gentle tapping on the door. The knock sounded like one that I already knew. I guess that's the reason it didn't scare me. My first thought was, what if it's someone looking for Will. My knowing self told me something different.

When I opened the door, standing staunch and proud was a tall man holding the hand of a little boy. The man smiled as he talked to me. He spoke softly and I didn't understand how I heard him over all of that storm noise. More than once he told me not to worry. He told me not to grieve. The man said there were some storms that would bring goodness and some that were just the opposite. He said they come in our lives to test us. He said, don't fail the tests. He told me that some storms come with living, loving spirits riding on them. Told me I'd already been through many and had learned the differences in them. Said I already knew almost everything. Somehow, I knew he'd keep speaking until I was satisfied. He looked satisfied too. But somehow, I also knew, there had to be one more thing. When the man and little boy started to walk away, he turned to tell me that one more thing.

"The time is right now", he said.

He had already told me that I already knew almost everything. Right away, I didn't understand what he meant. With my mind racing, I stood still, watching until they disappeared into a blast of wind and a torrential downpour.

Before I closed the door, I watched colorful streaks of lightening dancing in the treetops. I heard ear piercing thunder bolts. I saw water rising on the steps. I wondered how everybody else slept through all of that terrible weather and how I even heard that soft knock on the door above all of that noise.

I went back to sleep with that man and little boy on my mind. As bad as that storm was, how could I have let them stand on the outside? Why didn't I invite them in? How were they going to survive walking around in that fierce wind and rapidly rising water? My goodness! I thought, I completely forgot my manners. I wondered who they were and for a moment I felt I was back in Louisiana. With all those questions, I didn't understand how I allowed myself to go back to sleep.

I awakened from the soundest, most peaceful sleep I had in many months. It wasn't like I usually felt if I were awakened in the middle of the night. I felt rested.

The sunlight was so bright when I walked to look out of the front door that it was difficult to tell there had even been a storm. I expected to see tree limbs blown all over what I saw as powder dry land, but there weren't any. Strangeness in the appearance of everything I saw on the outside made me realize that I hadn't seen the face of either the man or boy, yet I knew they were smiling. The man didn't make sounds, but I heard him speak. That soft knock on the door reminded me of the gentleness of my father. I thought I must have dreamed the entire thing, yet I felt the message coming through, filtering itself from what I thought was a dream. What happened in the middle of the night, to me, was real.

I wrote to Grandma Caroline and asked her to send money to Miss Roxie's house in Memphis. I asked her to let my brothers know that we were going to Memphis.

"When are we leaving here? Clyde kept begging for me to tell.

"I remember Grandma Caroline telling you", 'Please be patient, Clyde'. "Do you remember?"

"Yes, I remember. Makes me wonder how we ever would have made it so far without Grandma and Grandpa."

"I wonder too. They have always been there when we needed them but we have others on our side too."

WHO! The only good thing we have is memories of when Daddy was alive."

"That's what you think. We have something better than memories around us. Daddy is still alive."

I didn't get the response from Clyde like the one she gave that day when we were in the cotton field and I told her I was surprised Daddy hadn't come with us and how I hadn't heard from him in a long time.

"Just tell me when we're leaving, Sister."

"I won't know until the time is right. Then I can tell you. I'll never let anything slip up on me again and I won't be disobedient to what I'm told. The day I laid my eyes on Mr. Johnson something told me he was going to lead this family to grief. I knew something was going to happen to John David and tried to ignore it. The last time before he died when I caught the train to Memphis and holding that fifteen cents fare, it was like it was burning in my hand. All the way there I wanted to get off that train and head back."

"Sister it isn't right for you to bear these burdens all by yourself. You should have told me."

"Believe you, me, I'm not bearing burdens by myself. I didn't want to tell you making you want to do something foolish. You would have hurt yourself trying to change what is destined. Besides, Daddy wanted John David to be with him. And, by the way, did I tell you that I know John David is alright?"

We talked until Clyde dozed. I wished that Clyde understood all the secrets. I wanted her to know what she was feeling on her insides. I wanted to tell her about the storm and that man and little boy. One day I would tell her but then, they were my treasures and my secrets to keep.

I was awake and busy the rest of the night washing, ironing and folding every bundle of other people's laundry. I had to have them ready to deliver before the end of the next day. I kept the sturdy pouch around my waist that carried Daphne's black braid,

Steven's wooden heart with our initials carved in it and the shiny gold one Daddy made for my cradle.

I worked steadily until mid-day noticing the afternoon sun was cheerful, not too warm and not too bright. I gave Thelma and Maurice light bundles to carry while Clyde and I lugged the heaviest. We delivered those bundles as fast as we could without tarrying after we collected the money.

"Slow down, Sister. We can hardly keep up. Now you're going the wrong way anyway."

I changed our direction when we met men with hound dogs going in the direction of our house. Changing my route made us have to travel through mud and swamp. The journey wasn't easy.

"Walk up, Clyde."

I didn't want to have to make them run. Clyde was already almost out of breath and Thelma and Maurice were irritable as children would be. It was becoming difficult for them to keep up.

"Run! Run! Y'all run!"

I could see ahead, passengers boarding the train. I had collected enough of the laundry money for our fares and had some left over. We were sweating, muddy and out of breath but we made it on board and happy to sit down. I laid my head on the back of my seat feeling relief only when the train pulled away.

Clyde pointed as she tried to catch her breath asking about undelivered laundry. I ignored her until she was curious enough to uncover, first one bundle, then the other, surprised to discover our own things packed tightly. She turned toward the window laughing and screaming.

"GOODBYE MAMA! GO TO HELL PAPA JOHNSON!"

When I slid down in my seat and covered my embarrassed face, Clyde screamed louder. She laughed until she was exhausted enough to sleep.

FORTY-THREE

When I was coming to Memphis alone to go to school, I always felt the warm welcome in Roxie Robinson's house. But the day Clyde, Thelma and Maurice were with me was the day I knew, from then on, I'd call Memphis my own. Roxie's hugs and soothing hands helped us easily make the transition from hell to home. She paid close attention to all that we told her. She asked questions that I never would have answered when I was going back and forth to Marigold. She was keenly aware of how mean and bitter Rozella was, but I never mentioned the things she'd done to me. I wanted to leave well enough alone. That's the reason it surprised me when I caught Clyde telling Roxie how Rozella beat me, about Daddy coming to school and Mama coming right behind him the very, next day. I wasn't ready to dig up all those bad memories. I wanted to bask in our newfound freedom, the Louisiana memories that were pleasant and the lessons that came clearer to me everyday. I admonished Clyde for revealing too much too soon. After all, Rozella is Roxie's sister.

"Sister, you told me, the way to move forward, out of darkness, we must first shine a light in the past. We must know what we're made of and take stock of all we've ever known."

Clyde's words made Roxie take notice of herself. For the first time since she left Louisiana, she began to let her red curls push through the black hair dye. Her true complexion began to show when she stopped layering her face with dark powder. After a while, she wasn't listening to us. She was talking to us. We sat on the porch together, talking, purging while allowing a light to shine in her past so her life could move forward. Clyde recited lessons. Roxie was no longer ashamed that she was the daughter of a red-headed drifter. She let the honesty of a girl, two decades younger than she lead her out of the dark past to the light of the present by reciting lessons from a loving father. I was so in awe of my little sister, my grandmother's namesake, Clyde.

FORTY-FOUR

The crisp, chilling March wind let us know that spring was lurking around the corner. Roxie and I put bricks at the bottom of the curtain stretchers to keep the wind gusts from blowing them over. The robust breeze made us work faster, one of us at each end, to get the curtains stretched over those sharp pins. The fine laced glistened with heavy-like crystals of starch in the sunlight. We didn't often look away from our task for fear of pricking one of our fingers on one of the sharp pins. That day, both of us looked up from our tedious task when we heard Carl's car horn. He got out of the car slowly which made me wonder where his enthusiasm was on a day like this when the earth was being re-born.

We made sure the bricks were securely holding the stretchers down before we walked to meet Carl. What other way was it for him to deliver unwelcome news except to blurt it out?

"Will left Mama for another woman. She doesn't even know where he's gone."

We walked to the porch where Clyde stood to listen.

"So, what!" Clyde yelled.

"So, she wants to move to Memphis. She said she wants to be with her children."

"When did she decide she wanted to be with us? We're doing just fine without her. What can she do for us now? She didn't do anything for us when we needed her. I don't want her to come here! Let her find another man to mistreat her. She likes that more than she likes her children."

I didn't want to add fuel to Clyde's fire but had to ask.

"Do you mean to tell me she's not somewhere trying to die over Will leaving her for another woman?"

"She's in Louisiana with Grandma and Grandpa."

"Well, sir"! Clyde sneered. "Where does she think she's going to live in Memphis? This isn't our house."

Roxie answered, "It's up to y'all. We can make room if you want."

"No! Let her sleep on the porch like you had to do, Carl!"

"Clyde, I thought you were going to forget that bad stuff."

"I can't! I thought I had forgotten it too, but this stirs all of it back up again."

'Honor thy father and thy mother. Forgive those who trespass against you.' "Don't you know we'd be asking for trouble if we turned her away? Rich, Ricks blood runs through our veins not crud and mud that seems to run in Mama's. We can't treat her like she treated us. Our rich blood is thicker than her mud. We have to stick together on this."

"I don't want to get any of her filthy mud on me."

Clyde stomped her foot and went in the house. Carl said he'd let her know it was alright for her to come.

It wasn't long after Carl left that I got a letter from Mama letting me know when we could expect her. Roxie and I waited everyday for a week at the Tennessee-Mississippi state line. I couldn't believe Mama was riding on the back of a wagon with her legs dangling. The old, dilapidated wagon was being pulled by an under-nourished mule that was driven by a hired man whose intoxication was clearly visible. The wagon was laden with cheap, raggedy furniture and rags Mama said she'd picked up along the way. The back of the wagon almost touched the ground. The sight made me remember when Mama told Clyde and me to stop acting like we were from the country. Well, well, well, I thought, who's looking like they're from the country now? Hidden among the junk were some of Grandma Caroline's treasures sent to me that Mama claimed for herself.

When Roxie saw Mama and the wagon, I could tell, she felt sorry for Mama and for us too for having to see her that way. Mama's head was wrapped in a tattered, heavy, cotton scarf that covered her baldness. Her eyes were sunken, and her dress was made from cotton sack fabric.

At first, Mama didn't sleep much. Like other times, she cried a lot. She acted like she didn't remember anything that happened after Daddy died. She talked about him all the time. She never mentioned Will Johnson.

Clyde ignored her. Thelma and Maurice were afraid to go near her. She was terrified of storms. I'd sit close and hold her hand when it thundered. She said she was afraid Daddy was going to come in a storm and take her away.

"Sister, what did your father tell you about storms? He didn't tell me. Did he tell you? Where's John David? Did your daddy take him?"

"Daddy was already dead when John David died. God took John David."

"He must have told God to do it. He'll probably tell God to take me next."

"No, he won't."

"Are you sure?"

"Yes, I'm sure."

Although I was still uncomfortable touching her, I'd put my arm around her shoulder. I taught her to make tea cakes again the way she'd taught me. Maurice and Thelma watched from a distance until they learned not to be afraid. I pressed her memory to bring her sordid past forward tempering her fantasies. After a while, she spoke less and less about Daddy coming back until she didn't talk about that at all. I couldn't help myself. Something within told me to love her pain away.

I'd never seen anybody who could almost die and come back alive as many times as Mama. She started doing most of the curtains and laundry Roxie and I used to do. She made her own money and rarely glanced toward a man. She looked better, started going places and doing things while exploring Memphis. One of those days, while out walking, she ran upon Bethel African American Episcopal Church. For the first time, I saw her working in church with a quiet reverence. She'd mention her children but not boastingly.

When Mama made enough money to move out of Roxie's house, she found a house on a hill. She bought pipe tobacco that she placed in a bowl and lit it on fire just for its smell. She'd come to Roxie's house when my brothers came, showing her displeasure at their disdain. I warned them and Clyde about the consequences of disobedience. Mama had forgiven herself and wanted them to forgive her too. They listened and tried but their superficial respectfulness was short-lived.

Clyde quit school to go to work where there was an abundance of men, at the Army Defense Depot, with Roxie. My brothers immersed themselves in the great, big, fast world of Memphis. Nobody acted like partners.

I didn't feel any of them feeling me and despite that, I wasn't lonely or alone. Something or someone was with me all the time. Under a watchful presence, I washed, cooked, cleaned and sewed while taking care of Thelma and Maurice all by myself. I went to school at night after they settled in. Once again I was taking on everybody's share but this time, I took on heavy burdens with a loving hand, a lighter spirit and an energy that I couldn't see that was helping me.

One evening after rubbing loads of clothes all day on that hard rub board, my hands were so swollen I didn't think I'd be able to hold a pencil to write in class. I was walking in the direction of the school when I felt myself being drawn forward by what felt like wavy currents coming from that mighty, muddy Mississippi River. I lost all control as its strength pulled me toward it. I wasn't strong enough to resist the invitation.

Reaching the banks, I was surprised by the stillness of something that was powerful enough to be irresistible. I fell on my stomach and submerged my stinging hands in the cool, soothing water. Somebody was watching that I'd have to get to know. It was a pleasurable feeling. I felt the kind of love I'd known only once that was with a boy with crystal blue eyes.

A breeze was coming from the north and so was he. I heard a baby cry before I turned myself over to sit up. He was standing over me as I looked up knowing, I was staring into the face of my children's father.

FORTY-FIVE

Eighty-eight years hadn't dimmed my vision. The older I get, the more I see. When I look at the night sky, I see Daddy's bright eyes twinkling in the stars. I see Grandma Caroline's smile glowing in the sunshine. Over my head I see fluffy, white clouds piling up higher and higher getting heavier and heavier with folks that I know, riding happily along. Mama even has one. It's a little bent but its right there with the rest of them. It makes me wonder how tall my cloud is going to be. With all those good souls crowding me, I'm really going to be lifted high.

For a long time, I could feel Aunt Daphne and Aunt Adeline were still on earth. Then when I felt their spirits floating all around me, I studied the sky and, I declare, I found their clouds. Grandpa Frank, Grand Caroline, Aunt Ida, Aunt Martha, Uncle Oliver, Uncle Stewart, Monroe, and Vee are all loving spirits by now. I can't tell about Walter, William and Starcie but Steven has never left me. Auntie Roxie is there still going around loving everybody.

Today, I sat in my window facing west as I watched one of those unpredictable, afternoon, summer, thunderstorms. I thought about my brothers and sisters who all left going in that direction to live. I thought about Maurice and what a fine man he turned out to be. He acts more like a Ricks man than my brothers. He didn't forget his lessons.

After the storm blew over, I walked outside, at dusk, to check on my strawberry plants, looked up and saw a strange rainbow. Its color was all blue and it stretched all across the sky. The smell of fresh rain on a muggy, Memphis, summer night brings forth the aroma of honeysuckle. The rapidly moving grey clouds rolled over a waning moon that brought on one of Daddy's lessons. With that waning moon staring down on me, the smell of a Louisiana bayou waving past my nose and remembering the unpleasant reason I picked up the habit in the first place, I turned south to spit the brown liquid out of my mouth. I vowed never to put snuff inside my bottom lip again.

I used to think of Roundsboro, South Carolina a lot when I first got to Memphis. No one I asked had ever heard of it, not even the people that came from the east. I don't have to ask anymore because that chosen child of mine reads maps, studies books and is now the one that asks the questions. One of these days that child is going to let a spirit be the leader, right straight to where Roundsboro, South Carolina is. I've already instilled in my chosen child how death can't keep a loving spirit away. That spirit might be mine. Nothing is ever going to harm any of them because I'll be around. I catch that child running those fingers through the grass looking for four-leaf clovers. Always finds them too. Sits at the piano, running those same, searching fingers up and down the keyboard arousing the spirits around us, playing and singing everybody's favorite song: "Precious memories, how they linger, how they ever flood my soul. In the stillness of the midnight.......".

My child has learned the lessons well, has passed all the tests and knows the secrets and mostly everything else. Knows not to tell anybody without Ricks blood about them. Is now teaching my grandchildren lessons. Has one that always asks a lot of questions and stares toward the east, I guess thinking about Roundsboro. My child doesn't have suspicious eyes because I've passed down the truth. Truth hurts sometime but lies will change your whole life and the only secrets they have to keep now are those that come in the storms.

CPSIA information can be obtained
at www.ICGtesting.com
Printed in the USA
LVHW090405290421
685801LV00027B/480

9 780692 037300